Fens End

MICHAEL ROUSE

2012

SHBB
PUBLISHING

First published in 2012 by
SHBB Publishing

A CIP Catalogue of this book is available from
the British Library

ISBN: 978-0-9571073-1-1

Typeset in Sabon 10½pt by
www.chandlerbookdesign.co.uk

Printed in Great Britain by
Ashford Colour Press Ltd.

DEDICATIONS

For Maxine and our four 'blessings' - Ben, Lauren,
Lee and Cassie; for ' Jack', that master storyteller,
John Gordon; and in memory of Sybil Marshall,
that most remarkable of Fen women.

CONTENTS

Monks Fen

BEWARE OF BOGGARTS & BOGLES

N
W — E
S

FLAT LANDS

MORE FLAT LANDS

Here be bugs, beetles and beasties

Monks Lode

Boathouse

Lavender Cottage

Willow Holts

Old Tom's Cottage

BEWARE OF THE DOG

orchard

LODE LANE

TO THE VILLAGE

Farm Yard

MILL LANE

NEW HOUSING

FENS END

Mike's sketch map of Fens End

1

JESS

'Are we poor now?'

For weeks Jess had known something was wrong. There had been endless, late night telephone calls and extra long meetings in town. Mum had been trying to keep herself busy, fussing with things she wouldn't normally worry about, and forcing a cheerful smile whenever she caught Jess studying her frowning face. The hushed conversations had been the worst. Mummy and Daddy hardly ever kept secrets from her, but lately they spoke in quiet voices and, if Jess came into the room, she would be told to go and play in the garden or read in her bedroom.

It wasn't until Marcie Whitworth had broken the news, her head to one side and a look of forced sympathy on her smug little face, that Jess had realised what was happening.

'I'm *so* sorry to hear about your father,' she had said, her mouth forming a perfect little pout, lips quivering as she tried to stop herself smiling. 'My father says that it is a sign of the times when a firm like Barnes and Jackson closes down.'

Jess felt her cheeks flush. Marcie had clearly been bursting to share this information with her and had chosen to do it in front of the whole class.

'What will your father do now?' He must be feeling terrible about losing all those people their jobs.'

Jess felt sick. So this is what the uncomfortable atmosphere in the house had been about. She had tried to take it in, wanting to give some kind of smart answer that would knock the satisfied look Marcie had on her face right off. And then stamp on it. But she had frozen to the spot.

'Oh! You didn't know, did you?' Marcie had given an exaggerated, drama-queen sigh. 'That's awful! Fancy not telling you, their one and only precious little daughter. I feel just *terrible*. If my family was going to be poor all of a sudden, I would want to hear it from my parents. You poor, poor thing!'

'So, are we poor?' Jess asked again, her father's face telling her all she really needed to know.

'What made you say that?' her father said, looking up from the papers he had spread across the table.

'Marcie Whitworth. She said that your business is closing and that all the people have lost their jobs and that it is your fault.'

'Whitworth? Her father's an accountant, isn't he? If it wasn't for people like him, we might have managed to get through this.' He sounded tired, his voice thick and angry. He pulled her towards him and put his hands on her shoulders.

'Dad, is it true? Are we poor now?'

'Much poorer than we were.' He took off his glasses and rubbed the back of his hand across his eyes.

'I'm sorry you heard it from your friends at school.' *Some friends,* Jess thought, remembering the look on Marcie's face, the sound of sniggering from the others ringing in her head. Her father drew a deep breath and continued.

'Time you heard the real story from us. The business is closing down this week. A lot of good men and women will lose their jobs. I'm sorry, but this house will have to be sold and we can't afford to keep you at St Augustine's. You'll have to change school.'

Jess swallowed the lump in her throat, trying not to cry. She felt her mum standing behind her, her hand stroking her hair.

'But where will we live? What school will I go to?' She had already passed the entrance tests for Nottingham Girls High School. Jess shrugged her mum's hand from her head and turned to look at her. She looked sad too, and she had dark circles round her eyes. Jess looked around the big room and through the large patio doors into the garden with its beautifully manicured lawns. Jack the gardener was working on one of the flower beds. *Poor Jack, did he know?*

'Look, Jess, love,' said her mother softly. 'Nothing has been decided yet, but one possibility is that we'll go back to where your daddy grew up. You remember Fens End? We still own Lavender Cottage. It was granddad's and grandma's home in Cambridgeshire. If we can hang on to that, then we will have a roof over our heads. A thatched one, too.' She forced a weak laugh, but it turned into a sob and Jess felt terrible.

'Look,' said her dad, pulling both of them towards him into a hug. 'We'll all be together. Think of it as ... going back to our roots.'

Your roots, dad, not mine, Jess thought later as she sat on her big, princess bed and looked around her large bedroom, with its pale pink walls and glossy white shelves piled high with her books and her favourite toys. She couldn't imagine not sleeping here, but forced herself to imagine saying goodbye to it. She couldn't. *My roots are here, in this house, in Nottingham.*

She had visited grandma once when she was very little. All she could remember of Lavender Cottage was that it was small and cluttered and there was a really old woman there who pottered around making jam sandwiches. *It was really good jam,* she thought. *But grandma must have been dead for some years now and I never even knew poor granddad.* She wasn't sure she liked what she remembered of Fens End. Flat and dark and wet and bleak. *Like the end of the world,* she thought.

She threw herself on her bed and hugged Tedder, dear ancient Tedder, until she felt like the stuffing from the poor, battered bear's tummy might start popping out. 'We're going away, Tedder,' she said. 'Away from here. We're poor now.'

Leaving St Augustine's and all her friends there had been really hard. Her real friends, Chloe and Emily, and some of the others had given her little presents and they'd promised they'd write and stay friends for ever. Marcie Whitworth and *her* friends stood in the background giving her horrible pitying little looks, while they whispered and giggled amongst themselves.

I could scratch their eyes out, she thought. *But I am not going to let them see me cry.* So she had left her old school that day with her head held high. And she kept it up high until she was well away from the school in the car.

'Oh, love! My love, please don't cry,' her mum kept saying, watching in the rear view mirror as Jess sobbed in the back seat. 'There's a lovely little village school in Fens End, and if you go there for the rest of this school year you'll make new friends. Then we'll find you a new school. We still have each other, you know that. We wouldn't let anything awful happen to you, we love you too much.'

Mum and Dad were always telling her how much they loved her. She was their 'little surprise'. They told her how, after they got married, they really wanted a baby, and waited and waited and nothing happened and they had almost given up hope. And then one day Jess came along and made their lives just perfect.

Jess had realised when she started school that her mum and dad were older than the other parents. Sometimes her dad, who was nearly sixty, was mistaken for her grandfather. Jess had never really known whether to be embarrassed or not when this happened. It was usually in shops, but her dad didn't seem to mind, and was always calm and just said very proudly, 'Actually, I'm her father,' leaving the shop assistant to mumble some apologies.

It didn't worry Jess that she was the only child. She had once heard some relative or other say 'she's spoilt rotten.' She didn't think she was. But she did live in a lovely big house and mummy had Mrs Baker to come in and help with the housework. They had an enormous garden and Jack, the gardener, kept the grass perfectly green and manicured, and there were lots of roses and trees. He always put her toys back in just the right place when he had finished mowing the lawns, and every year he would paint her Wendy house, and all the fences, and trim the bushes so they didn't grow too wild. Mummy didn't have to work and was always there for her, cooking lovely meals for her and her dad. She would help with any homework and drive her to ballet or gymnastics. They had lovely big comfy cars that hardly made any noise. Daddy worked hard, long hours and sometimes she wished she saw more of him, but like he often told her, he did it for the family and lived for the lovely holidays they spent together, staying in some very posh hotels, sometimes in gorgeous hot places with swimming pools and beaches and endless ice creams.

But that part of her life had come to an end. At the age of ten, here she was in dreary old Cambridgeshire. Or more exactly, Fens End. *Fens End.* Just a sprinkling of pokey little cottages arranged around a small village green with one ancient pub, The Feathers, and a few other cottages dotted randomly along small country lanes, with names like Lode Lane, which led down to Monks Lode.

'What sort of lode?' she remembered asking, thinking of a heavy load.

'No,' her father said smiling. 'It's lode, L-O-D-E. The lodes are a feature of this part of the fens. They are like rivers. Some people say they were dug by the Romans, perhaps for drainage or moving people and goods about. They are really canals, I suppose.'

2

LAVENDER COTTAGE

They had packed up their treasures from the old house, only able to bring a few bits and pieces with them because their new home was too small for much of the furniture. Jess had to let many of her own things go, taking them in bundles to charity shops and some of her toys to the hospital for the children there to play with. But she kept some of her favourites and most of her books and good old Tedder, who now lay on her little bed in the tiny bedroom tucked in the eaves of Lavender Cottage under the thatched roof.

'You'll be as snug as a little bird in a nest up here,' her mum had said cheerily when they first arrived. Jess had seen a blackbird's nest in the hedge at the old house, and that hadn't looked too snug to her.

She also wondered what exactly was living in the thatch above her head, imagining all kinds of scampering beasts that made her shudder. In the old house, she could hardly hear anything at night and there had been heavy curtains to keep out the light from the city. But here there were lots of strange sounds coming from the eerie fen close by, and it was pitch black as soon as the sun went in.

'A picture postcard,' her mother had sighed at the sight of Lavender Cottage, as they drew up in front of the higgledy-piggledy cottage when they first arrived. 'Just smell that honeysuckle and lavender, Jess.' The small front garden was crammed with pink and yellow and purple flowers and plants, climbing wildly up the fences and across the porch. Jess breathed in and sneezed. *Great. Hay fever. Perfect.*

'There's quite a lot needs doing,' her dad said, unloading the boot of the car. 'But some of those jobs will have to wait until we're settled in and back on our feet.'

The first morning, after a broken, tearful sleep that had left her nose feeling stuffy and her eyes swollen, she had been awoken by the crowing of a proud cockerel standing on a heap of straw in the small cluttered farmyard opposite.

'It's too early, go away!' she shouted and pulled the covers over her head, hugging Tedder tightly as she tried to get back to sleep.

Every morning that cockerel woke her up. Dad said it was better than any alarm clock, but Jess thought it was earlier than any alarm clock that she would ever set.

'Perhaps we could have some hens of our own,' said her mum, absent mindedly plopping some toast on Jess's plate. 'Wouldn't that be lovely? Fresh eggs, what do you think?' Jess didn't think it would be lovely at all, but said nothing.

The cottage had a long, straggling back garden with several trees, which Jess thought might be fruit trees, and she wondered what sort of fruit they might provide. There was certainly enough room to have some chickens and Jess tried to imagine herself collecting the warm, fresh eggs for her breakfast. But all she could think about was chicken poo and how the chickens would peck her hands. *Chickens, indeed!*

Gradually though, once the shock of the suddenness of the move had worn off a little, Jess started to think it might not be too bad here. Mum, and Dad were trying hard to make it nice for her and didn't seem to notice she was being deliberately sulky. So, one morning she re-arranged her little room under the thatch, sorting out her favourite books and putting them on the shelves in a handy alcove. She hung her clothes in the small wardrobe and put her shoes under the bottom of the bed. Once it was a bit more organised the room wasn't really so small after all, and the smell of the lavender and honeysuckle that had made her sneeze on that first day was drifting up through the window and was actually quite nice. *I certainly don't need any air fresheners,* she thought.

It was very, very quiet at Fens End. There was no traffic and only a few walkers who rambled past with maps. It was strange, but she soon found that she enjoyed the peace and quiet. It was lovely to be able to lose herself reading her books in the garden with only the buzzing of bees and a soft breeze rustling the plants for company. She was always surprised, when her mother called her in for some tea, how quickly the time had gone.

After a few days she grew bolder, and with mum and dad so preoccupied, she imagined herself as an explorer. So far she had only ventured to the fruit trees at the bottom of the garden, but when she got beyond them she was surprised to find there was some more garden. It was all overgrown but an old building made of dark wooden boards that stretched almost the whole width of the garden was just visible. The roof was covered in big orange tiles and looked a bit saggy in places. There were two windows, almost hidden by brambles.

After taking a deep breath, she carefully picked her way through the vicious nettles. *This is a bit like 'The Secret Garden',* she thought to herself. *And I'm Mary Lennox.* She paused for a moment and after a brief look back at Lavender Cottage, almost hidden by the trees, she thought that it hardly compared with Misslethwaite Manor, but then she remembered her parents, and how she still had them, unlike Mary. 'I will not be as sour-faced and spoilt as Mary Lennox,' she said out loud.

Jess reached the old wooden door and gave it a push. It was not quite a hard enough push to open the door, but the noise caused such a commotion from inside the shed, with a flapping and a scurrying, that she scampered back up the garden as quickly as she could.

I think I'll leave that to Dad, she thought. But her Dad didn't seem to hear when she told him about it. Mum said he was just worn out with all the upset over closing down the business and the upheaval of moving and just needed to rest for a few days. Jess wasn't so sure. He hadn't talked about 'going back to our roots' for ages. He barely listened when she spoke to him, and however hard she tried he refused to come and look at the old shed, preferring to stay in the house all the time.

Once he had shaved every day, put on a suit and tie and looked like the business man he was. They would entertain clients at the house and he would be full of conversation and jokes. Now he was unshaven and sometimes even sat around in his dressing gown all day long.

Jess didn't know what was wrong with him. He would sit for hours in a chair in the small back parlour. Sometimes he looked at the paper, sometimes she found him sitting in front of the television with one of those travel or cookery programmes that always seemed to be on in the day. He wasn't really watching it, she could tell. His eyes looked as though they had been switched off.

When she asked her mum what was wrong, she would only be told to be quiet, go to her room or play in the garden. 'Don't disturb your dad, darling. He's got a lot on his mind.'

He never came up to her bedroom now to read her a story. She was quite happy reading to herself, but she missed the way he used to sit on the side of the bed and put on funny voices, before tucking her up and giving her a goodnight kiss. Sometimes he had been so tired he had fallen asleep when reading and woken up with a start not knowing where he was.

She wished he would wake up now and laugh and be like his old self.

3

BY THE LODE

It was June and the weather was warm and the evenings long. Jess had started at the village school. Miss Matthews, her teacher, was very kind and the school was a lot smaller than her old school in Nottingham. She enjoyed having something to do during the day, because it was difficult at home trying to be quiet. But she would only be at this school for a few weeks until the summer holidays, and then after that she would be going to Soham Village College, a much scarier prospect.

When she got home in the afternoons, she would hurriedly change her clothes, gulp down a glass of milk and then go outside. She didn't want to disturb her father, who was often sitting in the same place he had been when she left for school that morning.

She was still unsure of her way around, but exploring kept her busy and her mind off dad. She knew the path into the village, but if she turned the other way they were the last cottage before the lane dwindled into a track beside the still, dark waters of Monks Lode.

Standing on the reed-fringed bank of the Lode, she could see across the seemingly endless fens. Apart from a row of electricity pylons striding across the horizon and glistening white in the low evening sunshine, the view was uninterrupted for miles and miles.

She tried to imagine the Romans digging it, like her dad had said, thinking that probably they had used slaves, standing over them with whips to make them dig. This lode was called Monks Lode, and she wondered if the monks had dug out there to bring the stone for the small abbey that had once stood not far away across the fen.

At school they had learned that the fens used to be a wild place. From what she could see from where she stood, the fens were still a wild place and a little bit frightening. But lots of visitors came to Monks' Fen, just over there to hunt for bugs or something, so it couldn't be *that* scary. Maybe one day she would go and look for herself.

The lode was quite wide and ran straight as far as she could see. Looking back, it seemed to go behind the garden of Lavender Cottage and some of the other cottages in Lode Lane. *It must somehow end along there,* thought Jess, *somewhere I can't see.* She didn't remember it coming out anywhere where Lode Lane joined the main road through the village. *Somewhere else I can explore.*

I could get a little boat, like 'Minnow on the Say'. Philippa Pearce was one of her favourite writers and she had loved 'Tom's Midnight Garden'. She knew that Philippa Pearce grew up in an old mill house and streams and rivers featured a lot in her stories. *Perhaps one day,* Jess thought, *I'll write a story about Lavender Cottage and Monks Lode.*

'There she is, Jessica Barnes, off in one of her dream worlds.' Suddenly she could hear the voice of her old teacher, Miss Gregory, so loud and clear that she was surprised to look round and see she was all alone on the bank by the lode. Not exactly all alone; a small rabbit was hopping along the tow path, before disappearing in the bushes and a couple of ducks were doing what ducks do best cruising along the still, dark waters.

'Hello, bun-bun,' she said aloud, and then quickly looked around to make sure no one could hear her. It was so different from the town to see animals and birds like this. She would have to learn to talk to the animals like Dr Dolittle. Now *that* would be something to let Marcie Whitworth hear about.

Why had she suddenly thought of her? 'I'm so sorry... poor you...' She could still see that face with its false look of sympathy, and it still made her feel horrible.

Lucky you are not here, now, Jess thought, *because if you were, I'd push you in the lode.* Jess looked at the water. It was too dirty and dark to be inviting, even on a warm summer's evening. 'And that would just serve you right,' she said aloud and began walking down the path.

She could smell the cow parsley growing in tall clumps before the bushes and trees that concealed whatever lay behind them. She could also smell... what was it? The lode with its fish, the rushes, the reeds? All of them, probably, all blending together to make a new smell called the fens.

Ahead of her in the reeds at the edge of the bank Jess could see a boat of some sort. It was long and low in the water. *Whatever is it doing here? Perhaps it has been abandoned.*

As she drew closer she saw that it looked like one of those flat-bottomed boats that she had been in with mum and dad once in Cambridge. They had been taken down the river past the colleges by a young man using a pole. She remembered how she had lain in the boat and dangled her hand in the soft water.

She wouldn't want to lay down in this one though. There were several inches of brackish water lying in the bottom of the boat. It looked un-cared for and abandoned, but she could see it was tied to stakes in the bank with two pieces of strong rope, one at one end and one at the other. So it hadn't drifted here or just been left. It had been tied up here, brought here on purpose by someone.

But why was it here, far from anyone? Jess looked all round and there, among the bushes and trees, set back from the path she was walking on, was a small, low cottage.

The garden was a jungle. A clutter of elderberry bushes, colourful lupins, sprawling roses and some bright white flowers that looked like tall daisies were all growing in profusion and covering the small windows.

No one could have lived here for years, thought Jess as she moved nearer, noticing a path leading through to the low front door which stood half open. *Someone else has been exploring here, perhaps other children*, she thought.

Jess hesitated for a moment, looking over her shoulder to see if there was anyone around, and then couldn't resist going up to the door to peer in. As she did so there was a low growl from inside.

She froze.

4

OLD TOM

hush, Faithful. Come you on in.' *Someone's living here*,
thought Jess, wondering if she should turn and run
away. 'Come you on in, don't stand on the doorstep,'
the voice ordered before she had a chance to move. So Jess
pushed the door a little wider and nervously peered into
the gloom.

An old man was sitting in an armchair near an empty
fireplace. There was a dog lying at his feet. Both were looking
at her. 'Oh, it's a little old gal,' said the old man kindly. 'We
just thought you might be someone else…never mind.'

'Sorry,' said Jess. 'I've only just come to Fens End; I didn't
know anyone lived here.'

'No' said the old man, looking her up and down. 'We
don't often get visitors here, do we Faithful?' The dog
looked round at the old man, then settled again at his feet.
'If we'd known you was coming, we'd have got out the best
china. I'm sorry I've had my dockey for today, so there ain't
much food to offer you.'

'It's alright, thank you,' said Jess, 'I've had some tea and couldn't eat any dockey, thank you'. Jess didn't know what dockey was, but she wasn't taking any chances. She shifted from one foot to another biting her lip as she tried to work out what to make of the situation and wondering whether to just run away.

The words 'stranger danger' flashed through her mind. And he was certainly strange, but curiosity was getting the better of her and she couldn't resist letting her eyes roam around the cluttered little room. As her eyes adjusted to the gloom, she could see more clearly an old dining table, ornaments, some strange looking baskets and large brown coloured photos on the wall.

A clock, taller than her, was solemnly ticking way in the corner of the room. It was beautiful. Through the glass in the front she could see the pendulum swinging to and fro. The minute hand clunked round.

'You like my ol' clock? Thass a beauty. A gran'father clock, that is. And that really is! My gran'father gave that to my mother and father as a wedding present. I don't know how he got the money together for it. But he did, and thass stood there ticking away all these years. Thass one of the family. All it needs is winding once a week and that'll keep you company for ever.'

Jess found the clock mesmerising, but the rest of the room was just as interesting to her. It reminded her of a room in a museum, but there were no labels to explain what everything was.

'There's a lot to see, some real curiosities an' all,' the old man said with a chuckle. 'You won't have seen many things like that, I'll bet,' he said waving his arm towards the baskets.

'What are they?' said Jess.

'Eel traps. Some calls 'em griggs and some calls 'em hives. They're made out of willow.'

'Did you catch eels?' Jess said, looking from the brown woven traps back to the old man.

'Course I did, an' my father afore me, an' his father. Thass one of the ways we lived in the ol' Fen. Eels, wonderful creatures. S'pose they're fish, a bit like a snake.' Jess visibly squirmed at the thought of fishy snakes, making the old man chuckle.

'They come in all sizes,' he continued, his eyes dancing with mischief as he warmed to his subject. 'Gran'father said he used to catch 'em up to a foot or two foot long in his day. If you haven't had eel pie, gal, you've missed a treat. We used to send a lot up to London. There was a man called Tubby Isaacs who was famous for his jellied eels.'

'The ol' fen boys, like my gran'father, used to believe the eel had wonderful curing powers. Gran'father used to swear, if you dried out an eel skin and stuffed it with lavender, thyme and other herbs then hung it round your neck, it would protect you from the Fen ague. My ol' dad wore an eel garter. Lots of 'em ol' boys did. Creatures of great mystery, them eels. They reckon there ain't so many about in the rivers now.' He shook his old head and looked away for a moment. Jess thought he looked a bit sad all of a sudden as he turned back to her. 'Still, hardly anyone catching 'em now, anyway,' he sighed deeply.

'Have you lived in this fen all your life?' Jess had moved a little closer, less nervous than she was before. He seemed harmless enough and she loved the way he spoke about the eels, even if it did make her skin crawl a bit to think of snaky things swimming about just outside in the lode.

'Not yet,' said the old man chuckling. 'The Ol' Black Dog ain't come for me so far.'

He stood slowly, his old bones creaking as he straightened himself and moved towards her.

'I s'pose we'd better introduce ourselves. I'm Thomas Fuller, known to most people round here as Old Tom and probably a few other things not fit for a little ol' gal to hear. This here is Faithful.' The dog turned to look at his master at the mention of his name. 'He's only a young 'un, but I kept him as a pup and then his ol' mother died, so we've got each other for company. And what is your name?'

'Jess – Jessica, Jessica Alice Barnes, actually.' She held out her hand and he took it, shaking it gently as he looked into her face, his rheumy, grey eyes narrowing a little.

'Jessica Alice, eh?' he hesitated. 'Barnes. I used to know some Barnes.' He looked deep in thought as he dropped her hand and went back to his chair, gesturing to Jess to sit opposite him on an old, wooden, upright chair,

'We've only just moved here, but I know my dad's parents used to live here.' She said, easing herself onto the chair, feeling a little less nervous.

'Thass a common Fen name, that is like Fuller and Bullman. Bullman was my dear ol' mother's name. Thass her over there. Jess turned half expecting to see someone even more ancient sitting on the other side of the room, but Old Tom was pointing at one of the brown photographs on the wall. A young man in an army uniform was standing proudly beside a dark haired girl in a long, light coloured dress.

'Robert Fuller, my father, and Eliza Bullman. That was when they was married in 1914. My father had just joined the Cambridgeshire Regiment and knew he was off to France to fight the ol' Germans, so they got married. A lot of folk did.'

'And that?' said Jess looking at the photograph next to it of an older Robert and Eliza, seated with a boy in short trousers and a girl about her age beside them.

'Mother and father and me and my older sister. Good looking ol' boy, wasn't I? He chuckled again, his throat gurgling as he did so. 'I haven't changed a bit, have I? I should think we wasn't much older than you in that picture. Old Tom Bolton took that in his studios down on Fore Hill in Ely. He were a good ol' boy, photographed everybody. They said in the First World War he'd been one of them fliers and took photographs of the trenches and all that. Don't bear thinking about, does it?' Jess shook her head, watching the old man, as he sat back in his chair, his head against the tall back, his eyes closing for a moment before he spoke again.

'My ol' father were one of the lucky ones, you know. He went right through the war. Got 'imself wounded a couple of times, but at least he came back. The ones that didn't are on the village war memorial. He paused again clearly thinking of the memorial and what it meant, before he returned to the subject of the photograph.

'I'd have been about eight, when we had that photograph taken, I should think. Long, long time ago, gal. Long, long time ago.'

'I'm ten,' said Jessica. 'I shall be eleven in the summer.' Old Tom nodded, looking hard at her again. He was looking very hard and there was a silence as she looked back at him.

She could hear the heavy ticking of the clock behind her. She looked at the old clock. 'I think it's getting late,' she said shuffling off the chair. 'My parents might be worried about me.'

'You'd better run off then,' Old Tom said. 'But afore you go, I don't s'pose your dad would come out here and talk with me, would he? I need to have a few words with someone and I don't see many people nowadays.'

'My dad? Well, he's...' Old Tom was frowning at her as she tried to explain. 'It's just that, well, he doesn't really want to talk to anyone.' Jess felt sad again and added: 'Not even me.'

Old Tom nodded, as if he understood, even though she didn't understand it herself. 'Well, what about your school teacher? Would he come and have a talk with me?'

'He's Miss Matthews, I mean, she's Miss Matthews. She's not a man.'

'Never mind,' said old Tom. 'But if you do know anyone, a man, that could come and talk to me, I've got a few things to say and a few stories I want to tell, before that Ol' Black Dog turns up.'

Jess ran home along the path beside the Lode. The sun was creeping down the sky and although she already loved this time of the day in her new home, she didn't want to bump into that ol' black dog Old Tom had mentioned.

She could tell it was going to be one of those lovely sunsets when you could see for miles and the edge of the world turned red. As she ran into Lode Lane she wished her dad would come out into the garden and look at the sunset with her.

5

THE SCHOOL TRIP

R ight, boys and girls,' Miss Matthews said in a loud voice. 'Stop what you are doing for a minute, put your pens and pencils down and listen. That includes you Alfie Carter.'

Jess had been busy working on a story. It was about a little girl, living in a strange new place and meeting a strange old man who lived on his own with a dog, but now she put down her pen and listened with the others.

'Thank you. I have all your forms back now, all signed, so we can all go on the trip to Ely. The whole of Years 5 and 6 will be going, so we'll be having a coach. It will pick us up here at the school at the usual time in the morning. If you could get here for about 8.30 it will help us to get everyone organised.'

'Now, we are going to Ely Museum to learn about the Fens and then we'll go down to the River Ouse and do some activities there, including a short boat trip. You need to wear comfortable clothes, clothes that your parents won't mind if you do get a bit of dirt on them or fall in the river.

Which you won't do, of course, because I'm not jumping in after you.' There were a few giggles from the class and Wayne Smith reckoned he was sure to fall in, but he could swim anyway.

'You will need to bring a packed lunch with you and a bottle of drink, nothing fizzy please. They say it will be a nice sunny day tomorrow, so we should be able to eat in the Park near the cathedral or somewhere in the cathedral grounds. You won't need any money, unless you bring a small amount, just a pound or two to spend in the museum shop.'

'We'll be back at school at the normal time, for those whose parents meet them. And don't forget, those of you whose parents are coming to help with the trip, remind them that it is tomorrow and they should wear some sensible shoes, because we will be doing quite a bit of walking. Now, return to your work and I want a good story in draft, please.'

Jess returned to her story and began trying to describe some of the things she had seen in Old Tom's cottage. She was aware of Miss Matthews standing beside her. 'You should find tomorrow interesting, Jessica – a good introduction to your new home here in the Fens. How have you settled in? It must seem very different from Nottingham, where you lived before?' Her voice had softened and Jess could tell she was being genuinely kind.

'Yes, Miss, it is different, much quieter, but I'm beginning to get used to it.'

'Good, good. Now Matthew Wilson what *are* you doing with your pencil?' She was gone in a flash and Jess settled again to her story.

The coach was big and comfortable. Children were pushing and organising themselves to sit with their friends. Jess hesitated until Miss Matthews steered her into a seat by the window. 'Charlotte, you sit with Jessica and you can point out some places to her as we go along,' she said.

Charlotte sat down and smiled at Jess. 'Good morning,' she said, in a fake posh voice. 'My name is Charlotte and I am your tour guide. Welcome to our guided tour of the Fens. There are three things you need to know about the Fens,' she said as the coach began to pull away from the school, leaving a few parents to wave goodbye. 'The Fens are flat, flat and, er, flat.'

As they went along Charlotte pointed out where she lived. 'That's it over there, and over there is where my Nanna lives, and down there, in that cottage behind the hedge, is where great Nanna Peachey lives.'

'Do all your family live in the village?' Jess asked.

'Yes, never been anywhere else,' said Charlotte, shrugging.

The coach rolled along the main road getting held up by the occasional tractor. She saw a windmill with damaged sails, some ponies in paddocks and vast fields of growing crops. Charlotte was right, everywhere was flat.

Suddenly, the bus swung round a slight corner and Jess realised they must have been a little higher than she had thought, for they were now going down a small hill and in front of her rising up from across the flat land, was the most beautiful building she'd ever seen. It stretched across the top of another small hill, sparkling in the distance like a fairy tale castle. There was a huge tower at one end and towards the other end there was an amazing structure with silvery white posts. The whole building was bathed in early morning sunshine.

'That's Ely Cathedral,' said Charlotte. 'Big, ain't it?'

'It's beautiful,' said Jess. 'The most beautiful building I have ever seen. It looks like a big ship'

'Well, I haven't seen many,' said Charlotte, 'but I suppose it ain't half bad. That's what they call it, my dad says, 'The Ship of the Fens'.'

Soon they were crossing a broad river with houseboats and lots of ducks, and then they were held up to cross a railway line. 'Ely Station, it's very busy,' said Charlotte 'You always get held up here. Sometimes people get stuck under that railway bridge, trying to drive through in big vans and lorries.' Charlotte giggled. 'Silly people! My dad says it's one of the most bashed bridges in England.' She shrugged. 'Nice to be famous for something, I s'pose.'

Jess looked out at the river with its narrow boats and railway bridge and view of the cathedral. Looking the other way, past Lee Smith's head as he bobbed up and down, she could see a long stretch of river and some rowers. This must be the river that Tom and Hatty in 'Tom's Midnight Garden' had skated on from Cambridge to get to Ely. She couldn't imagine the river all frozen over on such a warm June day, but the characters in the book had been just as excited at seeing the cathedral as she was.

The coach drove down a street where there were some buses and dropped them almost opposite the Museum. They were shepherded across the road and into a little courtyard where a small fountain bubbled away. One group was soon being led off out of the courtyard, while Jess's group of about twenty was taken into the Museum.

They put their bags down and were ushered into the room that was a bit like a classroom and sat on the floor.

A lady who said she was Sally introduced herself and then a man called John, who was going to sing them some songs. In the corner another man was chomping his way through a very large cream bun.

'And this,' said Sally gesturing towards the bun-man, who was wiping cream from his moustache and beard. 'This is Mike. And when he's finished his breakfast, he's going to tell you some stories. Listen well, because he knows everything there is to know about the Fens.'

Sally soon had the class answering questions about the fens and Jess learnt that the name Ely came from all the eels that were caught there – it was the 'island of eels'.

Jess was fascinated by the stories and even more so by some of the objects around the room because she recognised some of them as being the same as in Old Tom's cottage. There were eel griggs and John described how they were baited with something smelly like a piece of dead chicken or rotting fish.

'Eels liked something smelly,' he said, making some of the boys giggle and the girls squirm.

They fed at night and went into the traps after the bait. Once they were in, they got stuck because the twigs they had pushed through to get in closed behind them. Then the eel catcher would come along, lift the traps out of the water, take the cork out of the top of the grigg and empty them all out into his tub, ready to go to market.

Mike, who had finally finished his bun, wiped a dollop of cream off the end of his nose with a handkerchief, started to explain how there were not many eels left in the rivers now. *That's just what Old Tom said*, thought Jess.

'Nobody is really sure why the numbers have declined,'

added John. 'Eels are mysterious creatures. They are born the other side of the Atlantic and swim all the way to our rivers as glass eels. Then they live in the rivers around here for some fifteen years before returning to the Sargasso Sea on the other side of the Atlantic.

John sang a song about eels and how they could cure all kinds of ailments as well being sold for food down in London, where they ate jellied eels. Old Tom had told her the same thing, and she was still thinking about him when Mike began the story about a lad called Long Tom Pattinson.

Jess loved stories, she always had done. When she was little her father would read to her every night, but she wondered now if that would ever happen again. *Well*, she thought, *I am ten now, soon to be eleven and I suppose I can read my own stories*. But it wasn't quite the same.

The lights in the room dimmed and as Mike told his story, he put on a funny voice.

'*Yew, don't want to say the things yew dew, young man. If yew knew the things I dew, you wouldn't say what yew dew dew.*' It reminded Jess of Old Tom.

'*Well, you mind that Old Black Shuck don't get you!*'

'*He don't bother me nothing,*' the old man replied, '*he ain't bothered me for over seventy years and I got my safe-keep, so I'm orf…*'

Jess snapped back from her daydream about Old Tom. *What was this Black Shuck?* Mike said it was a big old black dog. *Was it the same one that old Tom was expecting?* Jess wanted to know more and she looked up at the storyteller. His eyes roamed over all the young faces staring up at him, but then he seemed to settle on her.

'*Well, I'll prove there's nothing out there, no boggarts or bogles...*' His eyes were crinkling at the corners as he related his tale, holding the children under his spell.

She knew this story wouldn't end up well for Long Tom as he boasted he would walk back home along the old path across the bog. Everyone seemed to be holding their breath, as Mike described Long Tom's struggle against the creatures of the fen until '*that ol' dead hand pulled him down into the bog for ever.*'

A sudden loud chord on the guitar that had been playing softly in the background broke the spell. The lights came on again as the children clapped loudly.

'Time for a short break and some dockey,' Sally explained.

Old Tom Fuller had talked about having his dockey. John, explained it was called dockey because while the farm workers were eating their bread and cheese and bit of onion, or 'hungin' as Mike the storyteller told them it was called in the Fens, the farmer wouldn't pay the workers' wages. He would dock their pay.

'Was that story real?' Alfie Carter asked.

'It was a real story,' John replied.

Jess waited until all the other children had left the room. She hovered shyly until Mike noticed her. 'Sally said you know everything about the Fens,' she said. 'Do you know Old Tom Fuller?'

'Tom Fuller?' He thought for a moment and Jess noticed that his eyes, which a few moments ago had been so bright as he told of Long Tom's struggle, now looked tired behind his glasses. She looked at his grey hair and his grey beard and thought how he had somehow looked younger when he was telling his stories.

'Tom Fuller, where does he live? Is he your grandfather?'

'No, I just know him,' stuttered Jess. 'He lives at Fens End, along Monks Lode Bank, in a little cottage. He's very old.'

'Ah, I see,' Mike chuckled. 'You thought I'd know him, because I'm very old too, did you?' Jess realised he was teasing her and relaxed a little.

'I met him the other day. He was talking about catching eels and the old fen, and you were talking about those things and I thought you might know him.'

'I didn't think anyone still lived along there any more,' he said, giving her a warm smile as he turned to John. 'John, do you remember a Tom Fuller?'

'Tom Fuller? How old is he? There was an old boy who used to come into the Black Bull, lived somewhere out in the fen, but I thought he was dead.'

'He is old,' said Jess. 'But he says he ain't going yet, he's waiting to be asked'.

Mike laughed. 'Is that what he says?'

'Yes.'

'Well, I do know several Fullers. I'm probably related to some of them. There was a lady called Sybil Marshall who always used to say, *We're all forty second cousins round here!*' 'Why do you ask?'

'Well, he said to me that he wanted to talk to someone. He wanted to tell his story, before the Old Black Dog came to get him.'

'When did he say this?' Mike looked concerned.

'It was just the other day. And when you were telling your story, I thought of him and what he said, and I thought he could talk to you.' Jess stopped for a moment, a thought popping into her head. 'He might have some stories for you.'

'You could do with a few more,' John said looking at the two of them.

'Yes, I certainly could. And you said he wanted to talk to someone, before the Old Black Dog comes and gets him?'

'Yes, that's what he said.'

'Well you'd better tell me your name, young lady.'

'Jessica Barnes, but I like to be called Jess.'

'Right, Jess. Tell me where Tom Fuller lives and I'll try and see him sometime tomorrow afternoon. He sounds like he's in a hurry. I can go out and take some photos if your Mr Fuller isn't there or that 'Ol' Black Dog' has already come for him.' His eyes were twinkling again.

Was he making fun of her? She couldn't tell. But he looked serious. 'Look you'd better join the others and grab a bit of dockey before it's all eaten up.'

It was a good day. Jess really enjoyed the little boat trip and learnt that the Great Ouse was a slow-flowing river like the River Trent, back in Nottingham, but it wasn't quite as big.

Thank goodness tomorrow is Saturday, thought Jess on the way back in the coach. I don't have to get up early and perhaps I'll go and see Old Tom and tell him about Mike.

As she fell asleep that night her ears were filled with the sounds of the night- time calls from the fens, and her head was swimming with the stories of those boggarts and bogles that Mike had told them about. She remembered that he had said that if you saw Black Shuck it meant death to you or one of your family within a year. Was that the 'Ol' Black Dog' Old Tom had been talking about? She hoped not. She didn't want anyone to die.

She took a drink from the glass of water beside her bed and shaking her head to rid herself of some of the thoughts she was having, she said aloud. 'I am not going to dream of Black Shuck or the Old Hooky Man who trapped children who fell into dykes and ditches or Dead Hands like the one that pulled Long Tom down into the bog. I am NOT!'

'Tedder,' she said, squeezing him extra tight. 'Let's dream of nice things like picnics or going to the seaside.'

6

SATURDAY

Black Shuck was standing before her on the path beside the Lode. His saucer red eyes glowed and Jess could see the steam coming from his nostrils. The evening sky behind him was blood red. She wanted to turn and run but her legs seemed unable to move and there was a cockerel crowing, a cockerel getting louder and louder...

Black Shuck faded away as Jess half opened her eyes to see the bedside clock saying it was 6.00. Relief that it had only been a dream swept over her, followed by the realisation that it was Saturday and she didn't have to get up yet made her smile.

'Thank you, Mr Cock-a-Doodle-Do,' she said, 'I'm not getting up yet.' She rolled over, made her pillow more comfortable and snuggled down for a bit longer.

After lunch she was out in the front garden when a silver car came slowly down the lane. She saw the driver straining to look at the cottage from behind the wheel. She recognised Mike the storyteller straightaway and her heart gave a little jump as he spotted her and waved. He drove the car up onto the verge at the end of the lane and Jess walked across towards it.

'Hello, Jess,' he said. 'So this is where you live? It wasn't too difficult to find, not many cottages to choose from down here.' Jess was grinning from ear to ear. 'You didn't think I'd come, did you? Well, I did. Thought I'd better beat the Old Black Dog to your Mr Fuller, if he really has some tales to tell. Are you going to show me where he lives?'

Jess led the way to the edge of the Lode and the path beside it. 'I love it here,' said Mike. 'Though I usually go over onto Monks Fen. I haven't been down here for years and years anyway. Have you been to Monks Fen yet?'

'Not yet,' replied Jess. 'We've only been here a few weeks and my father...well...' She bit her lip, remembering how her dad seemed to be slowly disappearing. 'He hasn't really left the house since we arrived.'

'Oh, I'm sorry,' said Mike. 'I hope he feels like getting out and about soon. Is this it?' They had arrived at the old cottage and just like when Jess had first visited it, it looked empty, with the door half open. Mike went up the short path and called through the door. 'Mr Fuller?'

There was a low growl from Faithful and then Jess could hear Old Tom's voice. 'If that's you about my field, I'll set the old dog on you.'

'No, Mr Fuller. My name's Rouse, from Ely Museum. This young lady said you wanted to see someone about some stories.' By then Mike had stooped through the low doorway and eased himself into the room. Jess followed behind him.

'Oh, yes, I remember the little ol' gal, she came the other day. Bright little thing, finding me someone from the museum! Now then, Rouse? Rouse? There used to be some Rouses in Soham at the forge in the High Street.'

'That's right, they were my uncles Willy and Ted, two of my father's older brothers.' Mike seemed pleased that old Tom recognised the name.

'They were good ol' boys, strong as oxes,' said old Tom. Then there were an old Rouse, man with a big flowing beard. He were a veterinary. He were well known around these parts.'

'That was Great Uncle Albert, my grandfather's brother. My dad was Ernest, known as Ernie.'

'Blast, I remember him!' Tom sounded excited, and he slapped his hands on the arms of chair, making Jess and faithful jump. 'He, used to come round after insurances, married an Ely gal, one of Harry Onion's daughters. Dad used to get his gates and ladders off them Onions in Ely. They used to be on Ely Market, in front of the old Corn Exchange, afore they pulled it down. That were a bad day's work, ain't many who'd disagree with me there.' Jess didn't know what the Corn Exchange was, but Mike was nodding in agreement.

'Come you in properly. Can you find a seat? Move that stuff off, just put it on the floor.' Jess understood that Old Tom had decided he liked Mike and she felt pleased that she had asked him to visit.

'Well, Onions, eh? Now that gal had a younger brother, Johnny, he were my age. Good ol' boy he were, always ready for a laugh. Loved his fishing. He was no age when he was killed.'

'He was 21. It was 1944 in North Italy,' Jess could hear the sadness in Mike's voice.

Old Tom shook his head. 'I lost some good pals in that war. It changed a lot of things.' He also sounded sad, and Jess wondered what they were talking about. 'I'd offer you a little drink, but I had the last drop last night and Mrs Clements, who fetches me a few things now and then, won't touch the 'evil drink', what with her being a chapel lady.'

'I'm fine thanks,' Mike said, smiling as he lowered himself into the old armchair opposite Tom. Jess sat quietly on the doorstep, hoping no one would remember she was there. She wanted to know what these stories were.

'Did you make the eel griggs?' Mike had picked up one propped in the corner by his chair.

'No, that was one of my old Dad's and I think his father probably made that. Gran'father Fuller grew his own willow just alongside the cottage here and he was a dab hand at making most things he needed.'

'You must be related to the other Fullers in the village?'

'I suppose so, way back, but I don't have nothing to do with them. I'm happy to live down here on my own, apart from Faithful here.' He patted the young dog's head.

'Your grandfather and father and you - you were all eel catchers?' Mike was still handling the eel grigg, examining it closely as he spoke.

'Eel catchers, wildfowlers, poachers, peat diggers, farm workers, the lot. We all was, but gran'father saw the best of it. We lived off the Fen, that was the old way. Course, thass all changed now. All the old ways have died out. Grandfather would take the gentlemen out in the old punt. I've still got that old thing outside there,' Tom waved a finger beyond the door of the cottage. 'He would take them out for a day's shooting and they would fill the punt with birds.'

'Gran'father would come back home with a brace or two and a few pounds in his pocket. They were good old days. I've got an old photo somewhere of gran'father with couple of gentlemen standing there with their shotguns and a whole pile of mallard, snipe and teal in front of 'em. They shot 'em for sport, we shot 'em to eat.'

Sitting quietly on the front step Jess looked out at the reed fringed Lode and glimpsed some ducks lifting off in flight towards Monks Fen. *Poor old geese*, she thought. *Poor old ducks,* she thought. *Poor old mallard, snipe and teal, whatever they were.*

'Father would bring home hares, rabbits, pheasants, partridges, all for the pot. My mother, bless her, could pluck or skin and cook anything. We grew all our own veggies out the back, so we didn't really go short, even in the hard times.'

'By the time I was starting work in the 1930's my father had got a job with the Great Ouse River Board. He told me he already knew that the old fen life was finished.

'How do you manage, now?' Mike said looking around the small room.

'Years ago, father got us connected to the water supply. Before that we got our water out of the Lode or the pump in the Lane. He got us connected to the electric an' all. Cost a lot of money even then, but I must admit he did the right thing. He said, 'You'll thank me for this.' And he were right. I couldn't be doing with lamps and candles now. Probably set myself and the old cottage on fire.'

'I've got an old wireless. I like the wireless, a nice bit of music - brass band, organ music and some of the plays, I listen to them.'

'Palmers still deliver my milk and young Johnny Fuller from Spinney Abbey – I s'pose he's a relation of some sort - brings me around some, sausages 'n' chops, you know. Lovely sausages he does. I like a bit of bacon too. We had an old pig out the back. We'd fatten it up with scraps and then get the butcher to come round and kill it. Kids would come from all over to watch that. Then, the butcher used to take some for payment and we'd have hams hanging out in the back scullery.'

'I've still got chickens, so I don't go short for eggs. Plenty of veg growing out the back and Mrs Clements brings me a few bits now and then. I don't go short. Mind you Charlie Plumb who used to bring me my bottle of whisky and some rolling tobacco hasn't been too well lately, so I have missed out on that.'

There was a pause and Jess could see Old Tom looking at Mike.

'I'll see what I can do next time I come out,' said Mike, understanding Old Tom's look.

Old Tom laughed. 'You'll come again then?'

'Oh yes, I think you've got a few stories to tell, Mr Fuller.'

'Yes, I think I have.' He leaned forward gesturing for Mike to come closer. 'And I have a favour to ask you, but that'll keep till next time. I een't planning to go anywhere just yet.'

'Well glad to hear it. Suppose I pop over tomorrow afternoon, Sunday?'

'Well, I shan't be going to church. Mind you the Vicar might pop round for a cup of tea,' the old man chuckled. 'Don't reckon we've got a vicar nowadays, not just for the village. Some city type bought the old vicarage.'

'You've seen a lot of changes over the years?' Mike said, pulling himself up out of the chair with some difficulty.

'Not all for the best either,' the old man shook his head. 'But I'd like to see you tomorrow, I think you can help me with a couple of matters.'

'I'd be pleased to Mr Fuller.' Mike turned towards the door. Jess saw him pause and look at the two photographs on the wall. 'Who's this?' He said pointing at the wedding photo.

'My father, Robert Fuller and my mother. She was Eliza Bullman. That was 1914 before he went off to France with the Cambridgeshires,' replied Old Tom.

'My father's four oldest brothers were out in France. Willy, was a Company Sergeant Major then came back to the forge, Alec went right through it all, but Bert and Clem were killed. Clem was only sixteen,' said Mike. 'Your father?'

'Served right through, got 'imself wounded a couple of times. Finished up a Sergeant. Hardly ever talked about it.'

'I don't think any of them did. Different times, Mr Fuller. A different world.' Mike looked closely at the photograph. 'And your mother was a Bullman, you say? My great grandmother was a Bullman. It's probably true, we really are all forty second cousins in the Fens.'

Jess got up and was standing in the small front garden among the lupins and roses when Mike came out of the cottage door, shading his eyes from the bright afternoon sunshine. 'You still here, Jess? You were very quiet. That's the way to hear things and learn things, Jess. Sit and listen. And I think your Mr Fuller has quite a few tales to tell.'

7

SUNDAY

What are you hovering by the window for, Jess?' Her mother had already asked her twice before and Jess had told her grumpily, she wasn't hovering, she was looking.

But Jess had been looking out for the silver coloured car ever since they had finished lunch. She wanted to tell her parents, but her dad had eaten without saying a word and then went straight back to his seat in the corner, and her mum was looking worried again.

It's just not the right time, Jess thought. Her mum would have asked too many questions and only have something else to worry about. 'What old man? What storyteller? Do I know them? Do you think you should be going there?' *No, best to say nothing, for now.*

'I think I'll just go out for a bit of fresh air,' Jess said.

'I would,' said her mother. 'Such a lovely Summer's day. You'll be shut in school tomorrow. Are you sure you haven't got any homework to do?'

Jess had her story to finish. But she crossed her fingers behind her back and said: 'No, Mum.' She was supposed to finish her story, but she figured she was getting ideas for the story from listening to Mike and Old Tom. Research, that was what she was doing!

Jess was watching two pigeons fluttering around in the top of a tree and wondering what sort of game they were playing, when the car came down the lane and pulled up on the verge.

When Mike got out he had a carrier bag tucked firmly under one arm. 'Hello, Jess,' he said. 'I've brought a few essential supplies for Mr Fuller. Man cannot live on bread alone.'

I know that, thought Jess. *And I know there isn't bread in that bag!*

'A little drop of whisky for you and some rolling tobacco,' Mike said placing them in the old man's hands. Jess had been right.

'Thank yer, thank yer. Bad for yer, I know, tobacco. But we all used to smoke when I was younger, afore they knew what it did to your lungs. All the old working boys had a Woodbine or some Players' Weights. The better off people had Senior Service, or some such. An' you'd see the old fellers with their pipes.' He looked over to Jess and wagged his finger. 'Don't you go gettin' ideas about smoking, my gal. Filthy habit. Coffin nails, they call 'em and quite right too. But an ol' timer like me, I think I'll take my chance.'

He turned back to Mike, who was looking at the old photographs again. 'If you could just hand me that little glass on the side over there, I might just have a small nip now.'

Mike waited while the old man rolled himself a thin cigarette and watched as he took a puff followed by a sip of the pale golden liquid that Mike had poured into the glass. Old Tom sat back in his chair with a broad smile on his face. 'Just the job,' he said.

'I s'pect the teachers at your school tell you how bad all this is for you, don't they?' He was looking out of the corner of his eye at Jess, who had positioned herself on the doorstep out of the way. She nodded. 'Mind you, bet they're not as strict as my old teacher. Mr Walling, he were called. He were a strict ol' devil, but we were a rum old bunch of boys he had to deal with. He was chuckling to himself as he remembered. 'Oh, he put that old stick across my hand many a time. I daresay I deserved it. That was the way then, His wife used to teach us an all. After she died, he married another teacher from Soham and they lived there.'

'Yes,' said Mike. 'He married my great aunt May, or Maisie, as she was known. She was one of the six daughters of that vet, Albert, you talked about.'

'Well, I never! Thass a small world round here, really. A good man, I think he was. But we hated them all. Couldn't wait to get out of school and start work at fourteen. My father had left school and was at work when he twelve and my grandfather couldn't read or write. He knew just about enough to sign his name. And not all of them could do that, they just made a mark.'

The two men seemed to have forgotten Jess was there, so she sat quietly on the front step, hoping they wouldn't notice her. The smell of roses and lavender in the air warmed by the afternoon sun was lovely. Suddenly she was aware of a nudge and when she looked Faithful had joined her and was lying alongside her. She patted his head and stroked his silky coat. He looked up at her with his big eyes and then put his head on her lap. *I've made a friend,* Jess thought.

'Sure you don't want a drop?' Old Tom was pouring himself another tot of whisky.

'No, I'm fine,' said Mike. 'Not much of a whisky man. A glass or two of red wine suits me'.

'Never did get into wine,' the old man said. 'It weren't the fashion when I was young. Mind you, we had a fair bit in '44 when we was coming through France.'

'You were in the army?'

'Royal Army Service Corps, but that's another story. Now, you know, I said there were a couple of things you might be able to help me with?'

'Yes,' said Mike. 'What sort of things?'

'Well a week or so ago, I had these two fellows come round. "Mr Fuller," they says, "Mr Thomas Fuller?" Well, I thought, there in't another one here. "Yes I'm Thomas Fuller." "Well," they says, "I'm Mr Something-or-other and this is Mr How's-Your- Father," I can't remember their names, but I've got a card somewhere up there,' he gestured towards the mantelpiece.

' "We've come to make you an offer," they says. "What for?" I says. "For your cottage and your land," they says. "What sort of offer?" I says. "A very good one, Mr Fuller, one that will set you up for life." A bit bloomin' late I thought, I'm eighty seven, a bit late for setting up.'

'Now, I thought to myself, here's two young fellers who have put on suits and collars and ties to come see me. Whatever they want must be worth a bob or two.'

' "Subject to this and that," they says, "we are prepared to make you a very generous offer for your cottage and land." '

'Hold you hard,' I says. 'Never you mind about all that. Where am I s'posed to live?'

'"We'll find you a nice place in Soham or Ely," they says. "We've got a number of suitable properties for you, where you can have someone to look after you. What family do you have, Mr Fuller?"'

'Never mind that,' I says. 'I een't going nowhere, except up the old village cemetery, when the time comes.'

'"You could afford to go on a world cruise, Mr Fuller," they says.'

'I've been abroad once,' I says. 'And all I got for my troubles was to be shot and shelled at. Thank you, I'm happy where I am.'

' "Well, we'd like you to think about it," Mr Fuller, they says. "Talk it over with your family. We'll leave our card and we'll call again next week." '

Jess saw Mike get up and move over to the mantelpiece, while Old Tom poured himself another whisky and began to roll another cigarette.

'You say the card is up here?'

'By the milkmaid. Won that at Ely fair on the rifle range years ago, trying to impress some young gal. Thass a nice ol' thing, don't suppose it's worth anything, but it means something to me.'

Jess had seen the brightly coloured figurine on the mantelpiece. She imagined Old Tom as a young man, probably with a cigarette in his mouth, leaning forward with the rifle and knocking down the targets to claim his prize. And he still had it, he hadn't given it to some young girl who had been hanging on his arm.

'I've got it. Jackson's. Big estate agents. What have you got here, Mr Fuller, apart from this cottage? You mentioned a garden out the back?'

'Come and see.' Old Tom got up from the chair and reached for a stick. Immediately Faithful got up and went to his master. 'Thass alright, boy, we're just going to the back door, but it'll do you good to have a bit of a run.'

Jess followed them as they made their way through a low door into a small scullery, where there was a sink and a cooker. The floor was just old bricks with no carpet or rugs. As Old Tom opened the back door, Faithful pushed through into the garden. *Another Secret Garden,* thought Jess as she glimpsed the trees and flowers.

'Thass mine, as far as the lane up there and as far as the line of trees over there,' Old Tom said waving his walking stick. 'And the farmyard over there,' he pointed to the left. It was the farmyard opposite Lavender Cottage, Jess thought. She could just see the chimneys of the farm house.

'Go and have a look,' Old Tom said. 'Thass all a bit overgrown now, I can't get round it all. Used to be able to once, but them days have gone. You still here?' Old Tom had noticed Jess. 'You'd better go and have a look as well. There's some good gooseberries on them bushes. Help yourself. I shan't eat 'em all, the birds will have 'em or they'll just go to rot.'

Jess followed Mike out into the jungle. There were tracks leading to a chicken shed where several hens were pecking around, and another track led to a vegetable patch, where Jess could see some beans hanging from vines. As they got a little further Jess watched Mike pluck something from some low bushes.

'Here you are,' he said. 'Try some'. He handed her several large greenish, yellow berries. Jess looked at them suspiciously. 'Nip the tails off and that bit at the top, that's what I do.' He showed her before he popped the berry in his mouth. He bit down and immediately smiled broadly. 'Oh, yes, can't beat ripe gooseberries, just picked. Reminds me of my granddad's orchard. I couldn't wait for them to ripen and used to eat pockets full of green ones and get terrific guts ache. But it was worth it.' Jess was unsure. She didn't like the thought of her guts aching. 'Go on. I know you are probably thinking it ought to be washed, but there are no chemicals on these. As my old Nan used to say. 'You've got to eat a peck of dirt before you die.'

She bit through the skin and the sweet mush inside burst into her mouth. It was delicious, a mixture of bitter and sweet. It was sun warm. Jess reached into the bush carefully avoiding the sharp, prickly thorns and pulled off a handful as she followed on behind Mike

As they moved through the garden, they found several trees full of small green apples and some plum trees with ripening fruit. A sudden movement in the long grass near her legs made Jess jump. It was Faithful snuffling around. 'Hello, boy,' she said and patted his head, but he darted off into the undergrowth in pursuit of something only he could see.

Beyond the trees there was an expanse of long grass stretching down to a wooden gate in a tall hedge. Mike was soon leaning on the gate looking up and down. 'It's Mill Lane,' Mike said, as Jess arrived beside him and climbed up on the bottom rung of the gate to peer over. 'There's been quite a number of new houses built along here lately, some opposite and in the field to the left and right.'

'I can see why Jacksons are sniffing around. This site is worth a small fortune. In fact, it could be worth a *large* fortune.'

They made their way back through the field and into the orchard. 'It looks like it's going to be a good year for fruit,' Mike said to Jess. 'I think the birds are going to have most of the cherries from that tree over there. You should ask Mr Fuller if you can come down here and pick some. Have you any brothers or sisters?'

'No, just me.'

'Never mind, it's just that they could have helped you reach some of the higher branches. Perhaps your Mum and Dad will come down with you and then you can take some fruit home and what you don't eat fresh, you can cook and freeze. Grandma Onion used to bottle fruit, especially plums and greengages. That's a greengage tree over there,' he pointed it out to Jess. 'You don't see many of them these days. They are really nice but they need to be quite ripe. My Mother used to bottle fruit as well. I don't suppose many do it now.'

'Granddad had three lovely Cox's trees and used to pick the ripe ones. I'm pretty sure those trees over there are Cox's. Best apple of all, Cox's orange pippin. A real English apple. Granddad would put the apples in wooden trays all wrapped in newspaper and put them in one of the old sheds, so we could would have fresh apples throughout the winter.'

They moved back into the small dark scullery and through into the front of the cottage where Old Tom was back in his chair rolling a thin cigarette.

'Well?' He said.

'Mr Fuller,' said Mike, sitting down opposite him, 'You could be a very wealthy man, you know that don't you?'

8

A WEALTHY MAN

A wealthy man,' said old Tom, blowing out smoke. 'How do you reckon that?'

'Your land goes right down to Mill Lane. Building land in a village like this is much sought after. That is why Jacksons have been to see you. Sell your land to them, or any other agent and you'd be rich'.

'And what good would that do me?' Old Tom was laughing and coughing at the same time. *He ought to stop smoking*, thought Jess, *it can't be doing him any good*. But she stayed quiet, not wanting to interrupt.

'Have you got any family?'

'Not any more. My parents had three children. There was a boy, Robert John, born in 1915. He were never the strongest of little lads and he died in that Spanish flu outbreak in 1918. They told me that killed more people than the Great War. It certainly killed a fair few round here. Poor little fellow, he's buried up the cemetery here.'

'Then they had, Sarah, thass her on the photograph there.

She were a couple of years older than me. Good looking girl, dark hair, like her mother. She found village life a bit quiet, always looking for something more exciting. She got a job in a shop in Soham and used to spend her wages at the pictures in Soham and Ely. All that glamour and romance, all up there on the screen. None of the ol' boys around here were quite good enough for her.'

'I were away in the army when the Yanks arrived over here. They were stationed all round here at different air bases and by all accounts, like a lot of the local girls, she soon found out that they could get her nylons and some of the things that were in short supply.'

'What was it they said about 'em? 'Over paid, over sexed and over here.' The local lads didn't like 'em coming over here and pinching their girls, but you can't blame 'em. They were young and a long way from home and those that were flying never knew if that day was going to be their last.'

'She fell for one of the fliers. He was from Ohio. Joseph P. Washington, the second. We used to call him G.I. Joe. His folks had some sort of ranch. I reckon Sarah thought he was John Wayne and she was going out there to ride the range. Anyway while I was away in Europe, she got married and went off to the States with him.'

'Didn't they keep in touch?' Mike asked.

Old Tom sighed and coughed again. 'They kept in touch for a while. Christmas cards and photos of the children. A boy and a girl. I think things worked out ok for 'em. Not as glamorous as she thought, I expect, but she stuck to it. They came back once. She was as American as he was, all 'shucks' and 'gee'. That boy of theirs had one of them crew cuts. But after mother and father died we began to lose touch. I've never been one for writing letters and sending cards.

'I got a letter from the daughter when her father died and the son wrote to me when Sarah died. That was some years ago, now. The letter's still up there somewhere. That was the last I heard from them.'

'And you didn't marry?'

'No, I never married.' There was a pause. 'I always used to say that I would get married when I had a thousand pounds in the bank. And do you know I got to nine hundred and ninety nine pounds many a time, but blowed if I could ever get that other pound.' Old Tom chuckled and gave another cough.

'So I reckon I'm the last of the line. Mind you, I think all us Fullers round here are related if you go far enough back. I can just remember my grandfather Joseph Fuller. He was married to a Randall from over Barway. Sarah was her name. Years ago there were more cottages along this 'ere bank and they lived a little further along. Nothing left of their place now. Father and mother moved into this one when they got married in 1914.'

'Grandfather had four children that grew up. There were some that died as babies. And there were others...' He went quiet. Jess could sense that the old man was thinking and when he did speak there was a strange catch in his voice. 'Well, things happened. This was a hard place to bring up littl'uns, a dangerous place and not much medical care then. We couldn't afford to pay any doctors. The local handywoman would come and help the babies into the world and the old uns out of it. Old Mother Edwards - we allus said 'Edduds'- brought me into the world just up there.' Jess could see Old Tom pointing above his head.

'She was a rare old gal. She made her own cures out of wildflowers and herbs. I used to have terrible ear ache when I were a littl'un and my mother would boil up an onion and when it had cooled a bit, squeeze some of the liquid into my ears. I think that worked as well as anything.'

'Now what was I on about? Oh yes, grandfather. As I said I only know of the four children that grew up. The oldest of those was Thomas. He was killed in 1915 at the Second Battle of Wipers. Poor old Sarah had three sons out in France. You've only got to look at the old memorial and see she weren't the only one. There were one family in a little place not far from here that lost five boys. Don't bear thinking about.'

Then there were Samuel, he was a few years younger. He was in the Suffolks and then there were Clara. I think she went into service and never came back and we lost touch with her. Samuel moved away, must have been soon after the war ended. He said he couldn't make a living in the Fen. There are some Fullers in Cambridge that we're supposed to be related to, but it's a common name. No, I don't know of anyone that you'd call close family.'

The old man went quiet again and Jess could hear the sound of another drink being poured. 'Sure I can't offer you a drop?'

'No, I'm fine thanks.'

'Ah, nice drop of stuff this. Allus kept a bottle of brandy in the house, but for medicinal purposes, as my old mother used to say. I s'pose if those estate agents have their way, I can have plenty of this stuff!'

Mike laughed. 'Look, I'll find out what is happening with the development in the village and call round and see you again soon. In the meantime, don't you go selling anything to anyone.'

'Don't you worry about that, but don't leave it too long. I've got a few bits and pieces to show you next time. But I shall have to have a good rummage around to find where I put them. Oh, and if you get a chance to pick up....'

'...a bit of bacca and another bottle?'

'You got it. Purely for ...'

'...medicinal purposes?' I know,' said Mike with a laugh.

9

FEN RUNNERS

Just the job. You know I finished that bottle you brought me only last night and I was thinking I hope you don't leave it too long before you come round again. And the bacca, much appreciated.'

Jess was once again sitting on the doorstep of the cottage. It was one of those lovely days at the start of the summer holidays, when the thought of six whole weeks off school seemed like absolute bliss. The sun was warm and bees were buzzing around the flowers in the garden at the front of the cottage, beetles were scurrying across the overgrown paths and butterflies were fluttering from plant to plant. She hadn't realised nature was so busy.

She had never seen so many butterflies as she had since moving to Fens End They came into the garden of Lavender Cottage and she loved to watch them, with their delicate colours and their flickering flight from one bush to another. Here at Old Tom's there were even more and occasionally she saw the beautiful dragon flies that came off the Lode and swooped around.

She had found a small pond in amongst the jungle at the front of Old Tom's cottage and she was amazed at the wildlife that hopped and bobbed around it. She had jumped nearly out of her skin the first time a frog leapt past her, but now she looked for them staying very still so she could spot them crouching by the water's edge, fascinated by the way their back legs suddenly sprung out as the frog leapt through the air.

She wasn't yet bold enough to try and catch one. Some of the village boys were really good at this and would bring them across to the girls and say: 'Do you want to see what I've got here?' Then they would open their hands and hope the girls would scream and run away at the sight of a frog.

Jess just liked to see the frogs hopping around with their bulging eyes on the top of their heads. And she loved the dragon flies that zoomed and flickered over the surface of the water, their huge wings so thin that the colours sparkled off them. She was beginning to understand why people went to Monks' Fen especially to study them.

As she sat there on the porch with Faithful resting his head on her lap and looking up at her from time to time, she thought, *I love this place.* She wasn't missing her old life anymore, and it didn't matter that there wasn't much money or the house was small. *This is where I belong.* But then she thought of her dad, just sitting at Lavender Cottage. Sitting in front of a television screen, someone babbling on and on, while he was miles away.

Where was he? Was he back running Barnes and Jacksons, making parts for industry? 'What do we do, Jess?' he had once said to her in reply to one of her questions. 'We keep the wheels of British industry turning.'

Well the wheels must have stopped turning, because Barnes and Jacksons had gone, and it seemed to her that her father had too. He hadn't even been to look at her new secondary school.

Instead of Nottingham High School, she would be going to Soham Village College. A 'village college' sounded small to her, but when she got there it was huge. The prefect showing them round said there were thirteen hundred and fifty students in the school. That was as big as some of the schools in Nottingham. *Some village*, she thought. But then she realised that students came from all around the area where she lived, including Ely.

It was all a bit confusing, but she liked the library, although it was called a Resource Centre. There were lots of books, especially story books, so she would enjoy that. The Art Department looked good and she loved what she saw of the Music block and the teachers there. There were some lovely playing fields and the old building that was the original grammar school. She wished the whole school was like that, but guessed she would get used to the sprawling expanse of all the buildings.

'I think you'll like this,' her mother kept saying. 'I know, it's all different, but this is a good school, with a good reputation, we're really lucky to have it so close to us.' Jess felt her mum was trying to convince herself too.

Poor mum, she's finding it even more difficult than I am.

Her last days at the village school were good fun, with a party and presents for Miss Matthews. Alfie Carter was full of stories of how all the new kids at the College had their heads pushed down the toilets and the water flushed.

'Oh yeah,' Charlotte had said. 'All of us? At the same time or one after another?'

'Dunno,' said Alfie. 'Just know that's what happens.'

'Well, they hadn't better try it with us. Ain't that right, Jess?' Jess had swallowed and nodded. She wasn't sure that she would be able to stand up for herself quite like Charlotte was.

A butterfly settled close to her and she wondered at the delicate wings as it fluttered by, wondering to herself what it must be like to be able to fly out over the fen and look at all the rivers and cottages?

'What do you think then?' Old Tom's voice cut across her daydreaming.

'Love them,' came Mike's voice, full of enthusiasm. 'Marston's of Sheffield. By Royal Appointment.' Fancy Queen Victoria using these? Well not this pair, but a pair like it!'

'I've lost one of the screws from the bottom, but the old leather straps are there. Don't think you could use them now. They must be well over a hundred years old.'

'Look at these, Jess. Do you remember the skates we had in the Museum? These are better than those. These have the straps.'

Jess took them from Mike's outstretched hands. Old Tom seemed to accept that Jess would find her way down to the cottage whenever Mike turned up. She was now his 'little ol' gal' and she loved it.

'Mind the...'

'Ouch!' She had found the sharp little points in the wooden sole of the skates.

'I was going to say mind out for the little sharp nail points that helped the boots to grip the skates, but I see you found them. You okay?'

'Yes,' she said. 'It's all right. They're lovely.'

'They were called pattens or ...'

'Fen runners,' Jess said.

'You remember that?'

'Sort of,' said Jess. 'You said, go and read a book called 'Fen Runners', by John Gordon. You said he was one of the best storytellers ever. So I did. It was a really good book.'

'Good heavens, I never realised anyone ever took any notice of what I said. I'm sure my own children never do. Yes, he is one of the best writers ever and yes, they are Fen runners or pattens, which I believe is the French word for skates, so must have come over with the Normans when they conquered the island of Ely after the Norman invasion and the defeat of Hereward. But, of course, you remember that, as well.' He smiled, but she was getting used to Mike's teasing.

'Of course,' said Jess, smiling back.

She looked at the steel blades, flecked and pitted with rust. She ran her fingers along the runner and traced its curve as it lifted up at the front. Suddenly she was back in Nottingham, at the ice rink. The best ice rink in the whole of Britain. The music was playing. Her Dad was with her venturing out onto the ice.

She was wobbling, nearly falling, pulling herself upright and clutching for her Dad. Then she remembered how suddenly she got it. It was so easy. She was off and skating. Really skating. Moving across the ice. Gliding.

'Come on, Dad,' she had called. And her dad was gliding up behind her, ready to catch her if she fell.

'I learnt to skate on the frozen lode when we lived at Fens End,' he said, breathless from keeping up with her. 'You never really forget it.' Fancy her dad, when he was her age perhaps, skating past Old Tom's cottage! She had sort of forgotten about the ice rink and how they could go there so easily, spending time together, laughing and racing and holding on to each other. She hadn't laughed with her dad since they moved to Fens End.

'Joseph.' She became aware of old Tom's voice talking to Mike. 'He was a fair old skater by all accounts. He was born in the 1850's, so when he were in his twenties, then you're talking about the great days of Fen skating. 'Turkey' Smart and 'Gutta Percha' See were getting on a bit by then. But 'Fish' Smart and his younger brother James Smart, they were champions and granddad skated against all on   'em.'

Jess recognised the names. 'Turkey' because he scuttled across the ice, 'like an old turkey being chased by a fox', and William 'Gutta Percha' See, so called because he was tough, like gutta percha, which was a hard type of rubber. John had told them about them at the Museum. And 'Fish' Smart or the 'Flying Fish' as he was also known, was called that because he was a good swimmer and not all Fen men bothered to learn to swim. Funny that, Jess thought, with all that water about in Fens. John at the Museum had sung a song about them.

'Gran'father weren't no champion. But he could allus bring something home for the family. Sometimes a bit of meat, or some prize money, or part of the collection.'

Jess remembered that John had told them how the skaters would 'pass the hat round' and everyone watching would put in a penny or two to be shared out between all the contestants, 'so no one would go home empty handed'. She liked the thought of that. She could imagine those tough Fen men setting out from their little cottages, just like this one beside the Lode and skating over to a contest. She thought of them trying their best against their fellow skaters, hoping to win something to eat, because when the land was frozen over, there was no work on the land and they didn't get paid.

Hard times. She knew a bit about 'hard times'. Things had not been exactly easy since they left Nottingham, but she had not gone hungry like some Fen children probably did when their Daddies weren't being paid.

Jess didn't like the thought of skating on the Lode. It was so different at Nottingham with all the lights and the music and the ice that was strong. The ice across those dark waters would have been thin in places that were hard to spot, with the Old Hookey Man waiting for anyone who fell in.

'I loved to skate, but my old father used to say, 'Not yet, that's just 'hard water'. Wait another day 'til that's solid.' She could hear old Tom again. 'Several old boys who went through the ice and never came out again. You were all right on the washlands where the water were only a few inches deep and froze solid, but on the Lode or the rivers, it were a different matter. Years ago, the winters were harder, we don't seem to have had a good freeze for years now.'

My father's great hero - was Cyril Horn. They used to call him 'Babs'. He came from over Outwell way. Outwell and Welney, thass where a lot of 'em came from. They'd skate on the washes between the Bedford Rivers. 'Babs' won four British Skating Championships and skated for Great Britain in two Olympics. I saw him skate a few times when I went along with Dad.'

'He was also cycling champion of England. So was his younger brother, Dennis. They even had their pictures on cigarette cards. Do you remember them?' Mike nodded.

'We all collected 'em, the men would give the cards to us old boys.'

Old Tom rolled another cigarette and sank back into his chair. 'So,' he said smiling as the smoke drifted round his head. 'They want my land for houses?'

'They certainly do,' said Mike. 'Building plots in the village are very hard to come by and they can get several houses on that top end off Mill Lane and probably some more if they push hard enough.'

'Well, I int gonna sell. And I'll drink to that.'

10

WATER, WATER, EVERYWHERE

'm making as many notes as I can of Old Tom's stories. There could be a book there, eventually,' Mike said to Jess one day as they walked along beside the lode.

'He said he'd find something else for me to look at today. He keeps finding some extraordinary things.'

'I loved the skates,' Jess said.

'Did you go skating at Nottingham Ice Rink?'

'Daddy took me there several times. I used to love it with all the music playing, but I don't think I would like to skate on there.' Jess was looking at the Lode pretending to be concentrating on that. But really she was thinking about her dad again and sort of wished Mike hadn't mentioned skating as they had so much fun together back then.

'Don't think I would either. Not that I can skate. My children would though, they can all skate. They frighten me at times, they seem so fearless.'

When they reached the cottage, Faithful came out to greet them both wagging his tail.

'Glad the pair of you've come out,' Old Tom said, 'cos I've got something to show you. Do you know what these are?' He handed out a couple of spades or shovels.

'This one,' Mike said looking at one with a heart shaped blade. 'Is this a sharp shovel?'

'Thass the one!' Old Tom was pleased. 'They also called that a hodding spade. You used them for all sorts of digging drains or cutting turves. You know what the other one is?'

'It's a slubbing spade or scoop,' Mike said admiring it. ' Lovely and light. Look at this Jess. It is made of wood and this would scoop the mud and water out of drains and ditches. You see how it is shaped and curved so it will hold the slub?' Jess looked confused.

'Don't you remember? John said it was one of his favourite words. Great fen word - slub, a mixture of mud and water.'

'In gran'father's time they used to have gangs of navvies cutting and clearing out the drains. Eventually dredgers did the work. There'd be gangs out puddling the banks to keep them high and waterproof. There'd be barges full of clay and the men would shovel it out and build up the bank and smooth it out. They used the back of that scoop. See, it's got a curve on it. Useful tool that.'

'Your grandfather must have seen a lot of the drainage windmills that still stood around the Fens.'

'I imagine so. I know there were some good old mills over on Soham Mere, but I don't recall any of them.'

'You remember, Jess, how the peat shrank and they had to build banks to keep the water in the rivers.'

'Banks of clay,' Jess said.

'So you were listening! Yes, when they started having to lift the water from the fens into the rivers, hundreds of windmills were built to do it.'

'They used to say the ol' fen shrank – 'the height of a man, the life of a man,' Old Tom added.

'Certainly some parts of the fens are now five or six feet below sea level. Think of that,' said Mike, 'the water would be over your head, Jess!'

'The old fen boys, the real old Fen Tigers,' Old Tom said with a glint in his eyes, 'didn't want no drainage at all. Their livelihood was fishing, wildfowling and the like. They used to break banks down. They were a rough old lot, near savages some of them. Thass why some of that Fen over there was never drained.'

Two shadows in the door of the cottage made Mike, Jess, Old Tom and Faithful turn to look. Faithful began to growl. 'S all right, boy.' Old Tom put a hand on him.

'Mr Fuller?' A well-spoken voice came from the taller of the two figures. 'Oh, sorry, you have visitors here?' He stepped further in to the room while his colleague was stuck in the doorway.

'Ah,' said Old Tom. 'The gents in suits, who want to buy my land.'

'We said we'd come back to see you, after you've had time to think it over.'

Mike stood up. 'You must be?'

'Jeremy Russell-Shaw,' the man said.

'Mike Rouse,' Mike said offering his hand. 'I represent Mr Fuller.'

Russell-Shaw hesitated. 'We had hoped to talk to Mr Fuller himself.'

'Anything you want to say to me, you can say to Mr Rouse 'ere,' Old Tom said with one of his slow smiles.

Mr Russell-Shaw paused and took a sharp breath, clearly giving himself a moment to assess a situation that he disapproved of. 'Since we first came here, my colleague and I have agreed that Mr Fuller may continue to live in this cottage, if we could acquire the orchard. We are prepared to offer a very good price. Mr Fuller would then have a nice sum of money to make himself comfortable in his later years.'

'Mr Fuller has very modest needs,' said Mike, 'He really is not interested in selling.'

'If you should reconsider, Mr Fuller, you have our card.' Russell–Shaw peered around Mike to look at Old Tom, unhappy that a go-between was speaking on the old man's behalf.'

'Well I won't,' Old Tom said firmly.

'Thank you,' Mike said, politely ushering Russell-Shaw towards the door where he became tangled with his colleague, the pair of them tumbling out into the front garden.

'Who'd have thought my land could be worth so much money, as to bring the likes of them round.' Old Tom tutted in disbelief and scratched his head. 'I mean when I were young, this old cottage used to get flooded out most winters.'

'What did you do?' Jess looked alarmed.

'Well father allus 'ad some large old bits of wood so we'd put some of the furniture up on 'em and just carry on. Course we slept upstairs, so that were alright. When the water went down we'd get the old garden broom out and sweep the slub down between the floor bricks. This floor is only bricks laid on soil.'

'There isn't as much flooding now in the Fens is there? Everything is so well drained and managed now. There hasn't been any major flooding since 1947,' Mike said as he came back in after watching the two men in suits leave.

'1947? That were a cruel winter. Father was there working for the River Board and I'd just come home out of the army. I hadn't seen so much snow and ice for years. Talk about a homecoming! Father was over Haddenham way. They 'ad a terrible battle on their hands. "The Battle of the Banks" it was called later.

'When it was at its worst, there were regular army and German prisoners of war, from the prisoner-of-war camp at Ely working side by side. Father said they were good ol' boys, but I found that difficult, after what I'd seen during the war. You see father had been through the First World War and he had a great respect for the Germans they were fighting against.'

'He used to say, they were just ordinary young lads like us and it weren't their fault, anymore than it were ours. It was the politicians.' He seemed to have drifted off for a moment, his eyes focusing on something Jess couldn't see. *Looking into the past, I suppose*, she thought.

'There's only a few places, like over on Monks' Fen, where you get some idea of what the old fens were like.' Old Tom was back, concentrating on the matter in hand again. 'It took a lot of cutters, navvies, slubbers and puddlers to make that land out there what it is today. And my little old bit of it is worth a bob or two? Well, I'm blowed'.

11

SUMMER HOLIDAYS

Jess would have liked to see some of her old friends during the school holiday, but it wasn't possible. Her father didn't want to drive anywhere and they couldn't come and stay while he was behaving so strangely.

Jess had plucked up the courage to ask her mother if maybe dad was poorly and should see a doctor, but she just said: 'He'll be all right in time.'

We've been here six weeks already, how much time will it take? The realisation that she had been at Fen End for only six weeks took her aback. It seemed so much longer. *Good job I found Old Tom and Mike. I'd have been very lonely otherwise.*

When she finally broached the subject of her new friends, her mother had been a bit worried and suspicious. 'Who are they? Are they all right? How did you meet them?'

'Of course they're all right, Mum,' she had said. Old Tom is an old man and he has a dog. Mike is the storyteller at Ely Museum, and I'm a big girl now and getting used to looking after myself.' The last words didn't come out quite right and she could see that her mum was a little shaken. For a moment, Jess thought they were going to talk about things, but then her mum just sighed and nodded her head.

'Well, if you're sure,' she said.

Jess enjoyed visiting Old Tom. He knew so much about the olden days and he said such strange things. When the dark clouds were gathering over the Fen one day he said to her, 'It looks like it's going to rain over Will's mother's,' and she never could work out who Will was, let alone where his mother was.

One day he had taken her out through the scullery and pointed out a door to her. 'If you ever need to... you know, there's a proper toilet in there,' he said with some pride. 'Not what I had to put up with when I was your age.'

Jess looked at him. 'Well in the evenings, not like today with all this electrickery, you might have an oil lamp downstairs, sometimes you took a candle with you up stairs. I used to hate it if I needed to go toilet when it was dark or at night. We had a little outhouse round the back. We called it a 'bucket and chuck it'. There was a wooden bench with two holes in it, one for adults and one for children and there were buckets underneath that you had to empty when they were getting full and bury the waste in the garden. As a child I hated sitting next to that big hole, I was always afraid of falling down it. I'd try and take a candle out there with me, but it always blew out and then I could feel the old rats running around over my feet. I hated that.' He shuddered and so did Jess at the very thought of it.

'Many a cottage had an earth closet, just a little wooden hut, with a seat over a hole in the ground. When the hole was full you just filled it in and moved the hut. Jess was horrified. All she could think about was how bad it must have smelled and how uncomfortable it must have been. She pulled a face.

'Hah! You think that were bad,' said Old Tom, enjoying her discomfort. 'Some didden even have that. The family just went broadcast! Just ducked down in the fields. Even we were better off than that!'

'How lucky we are today to have electric lights, indoor toilets and taps for water,' said Jess thoughtfully.

Old Tom smiled at her. 'I'm glad even a littl'un like you appreciates that, my gal. They weren't always such good ol' days.'

Jess had begun taking Faithful for walks along the Lode bank. Although really it was more like Faithful taking Jess for a walk as he scampered about, diving in and out of the undergrowth and dashing off into the reeds to worry the ducks.

He was also very good at chasing the rabbits, though so far with her, he had not caught one. When she told Old Tom, he grinned and said, 'When he does get one, you want to take it home for the pot. Get your mother to make a nice rabbit stew with some onions and carrots. Just the job.'

She couldn't imagine that her mother knew anything about taking the fur and skin off a rabbit, even if she knew how to cook it.

Now she was getting bolder, and with Faithful leaping ahead they went further every day. One warm afternoon they got as far as the top of Monks Lode where it joined a larger river, straight and man made. From here she could see across the whole Fen, across the meadows and lakes to the edges of distant villages. She could see the white sails of a windmill and a path and a bridge and there were some cyclists exploring the fen. *I want to do that*, she thought, *on a nice day like today.* The night time fens still frightened Jess. It seemed like such a lonely and dangerous place. And she still wasn't sure if she believed they were full of boggarts and bogles, so she wasn't ready to take a chance yet.

She had found a solid wooden seat placed precisely to look out across the fen. She went to sit on it while Faithful ran up and down snuffling through the long grass. There was an inscription carved in the wood: 'In loving memory of Robert and Alice Barnes'. *Alice was my grandma, this could be one of my special places.*

Jess had already made a special place for herself in the front garden of Lavender Cottage. She had found an old chair and set it up near a big heavily scented red rose bush. Nearby there was some lavender, trailing sweet peas and honeysuckle creeping up over an old tree stump. The gorgeous, heady smells reminded her of some of perfume counters in the posh shops. It was lovely to just sit there in the sun, losing herself in a story.

At the moment she was re-reading some of her Jacqueline Wilson books. When she felt sad, she often thought that Jacqueline Wilson could write a story about her and what had happened to her in the last few weeks. She knew she was not Tracey Beaker, but her life lately was like a story. *Maybe one day I'll write it down myself for other little girls to read.*

She could see it now. 'If you would just sign here, Miss Barnes. Put, 'to Lucy'. Thank you so much, Miss Barnes. We did enjoy your last book…' She was so absorbed in her daydream that she didn't see Mike's car pulling up or notice that he wasn't alone.

She looked up just in time to see a blond haired boy, possibly a little older than her, literally tumbling out of the car. He rolled down the verge and finished sitting in the middle of the dusty lane. He was getting up and wiping some of the dust off with his hands, when Mike got out of the car and saw Jess. She was staring at the spectacular arrival.

12

SOME COMPANY

Mike came across. 'Hello, Jess. I didn't tell you that I had a son, only a little bit older than you, did I? Meet Lee.'

'Hello', said Lee brushing his long blond hair from his face and immediately leaving a great smudge of dirt across his nose and forehead. 'Do you live here? Can I have look round?'

'Hold on, maybe Jess has other things she wants to do and not have you all over the place,' Mike said, gently holding him back.

'No, it's fine,' said Jess, still staring at this strange animated boy who was now pulling the heads off the lavender and flicking them in all directions. 'We can't go in the house, though, because my Dad's in there.'

'What's wrong with him? Never mind. Have you got a big garden? I want to see it.' He was off before either of them could stop him.

'I'm just popping some essential supplies down to Old Tom. Are you sure it's ok if he plays here for a while?

I won't be too long and you know where I am if you need me. Lee wanted to come along for the ride. He gets easily bored during the holidays. I thought you might like a bit of company.'

How could she say no? Anyway, it was company. Lively company at that. And just the sort of company who would love to help her explore the garden and the old shed.

'It's fine,' smiled Jess, thinking how the shed would seem far less scary if there was someone else with her. 'Lee can help me look at the old shed at the bottom of the garden. I haven't dared go in there yet.'

'Show me where it is,' came Lee's voice, although she wasn't sure where he was. 'I love exploring. See you, Dad.'

Before she could say anything, Lee was going through the gate that led to the back of the cottage. As they went round her mother was standing by the back door.

'Oh, hello, love. Is this a friend from the village?' She asked.

'I'm Lee,' he said offering a rather dirty hand out to be shaken. 'I live in Ely. I'm here with my dad, although he's gone to take some things to someone. I love your garden.' With that he was off. Jess looked at her mother, who was looking a little dazed, gave a little smile and then set off after Lee.

'You've got more trees than we have,' he yelled over his shoulder. 'We're going to have a lot of apples this year, so are you. Plums, great!' He picked up some of the windfalls and threw them further down the garden, while stuffing another one into his mouth.

Jess turned to look back at her mother. This was the first person who had visited her at the house and he wasn't exactly a friend. Her mother had gone back into the cottage.

When she turned round Lee had gone. 'Lee? Lee?'

'You should build a tree house up here,' came the reply from somewhere overhead. When she looked up, she saw a pair of trainers hanging below the branch of one of the large trees that formed part of the hedge at the side of the garden. 'This is a great tree for it. It's really strong.'

There was a sudden sharp cracking sound and Lee came falling down, landing just a few feet in front of her clutching a broken branch. 'Are you all right?' Jess asked rushing forward to help him.

'Sure. Stupid branch. That one was rotten. The rest of the tree is really strong. I mean it. You could build a really good tree house up there. I think I've broken my leg.'

'What!' Jess said. 'You haven't. Have you?'

'Feels like it,' said Lee. 'What's in that shed?' He had seen the old building at the bottom of the garden and he was up and moving towards it. He was limping. 'Ouch! Ouch!' he said.

'It can't be broken,' she said, catching up with him.

'What can't?'

'Your leg? You wouldn't be able to walk at all if it was broken.'

'Oh, that, no. But it really hurts though. What's in here?' He was at the door of the long shed, at the point she had previously reached, but had turned away feeling scared.

'I don't know,' she said, feeling a little nervous as she remembered all the creepy sounds she had heard.

'What do you mean? Haven't you been in?' Lee looked at her in disbelief, hands on his hips, head to one side.

'No. I've only lived here a few weeks,' said Jess, sounding a little defensive.

'Oh,' he said, no longer bothered. 'I thought you'd lived here for years. It's not locked is it?' He pulled at the door and it started to open. Jess could hear the fluttering from inside. 'Something in there,' he said.

Before she could reply, he had somehow armed himself with a stout piece of branch and was heaving the old door wide open. 'Oh, wow, look at this!'

Jess went forward, cautiously, to join him in the open doorway. She had been expecting a dark old shed, but there was light streaming in from the other side. Part of it was open and some pigeons were flapping away out of the shed through a large opening.

The children just stood blinking as their eyes adjusted to the sight. 'There's a sort of boat,' Lee said.

Jess was trying to take it all in. It must be a kind of boat house, because there was definitely a long boat, like the one moored near Old Tom's, pulled up in part of the shed. As her eyes grew more accustomed to the light, she could make out reeds and rushes through the opening beyond the boat. *It must be the Lode*, she thought. She had already worked out that the Lode ran behind the cottage somewhere, but she hadn't realised that her garden ran down to it.

The floor of the old building was covered in dirt and duck mess. *No one has been in here for years and years,* she thought. She looked up and there were old rafters hanging in cobwebs. On one wall she could see old tools hanging up, some spades and bits and pieces. And on the other side there was a pile of old nets.

For a few moments, even Lee was quiet and still, just taking it all in. She thought that they must have felt like this when they first saw inside Tutankhamen's tomb.

She had learned about the Ancient Egyptians for a project at her old school. But this was all hers. She wanted to rush up the garden path and say to mum and dad: 'Do you know what is at the bottom of our garden?' but she knew that it would be a waste of time.

'I've seen one of these before,' Lee was standing beside her holding a strange looking spade.

Jess looked. So had she, at the Museum the other week. It was like a spade, but had a special bit on the bottom that helped the turf cutter cut out the blocks of peat.

'It's for cutting peat,' said Jess. 'It's got a special name, your Dad will know, I've forgotten.'

'So have I,' said Lee. He was moving further around the old shed. 'There's lots of tools and nets and things,' he said.

Jess followed him carefully. The floor of the shed was squishy under her feet. She hated to think what she was treading in but at least it all seemed dry. They reached the opening on the other side and looked through. Nettles and grass, grew all over the path, but she realised she was on the bank of the Lode. She could see the dark water with weed covering some of it and the remains of some sort of landing stage. She wouldn't have liked to have trodden on some of those boards, they looked too rotten.

'And you didn't know this was here at the bottom of your garden?' Lee was giving her his disbelieving look again.

'No, I told you, I haven't been down here before.'

'You lucky thing. Fancy having your own river. And a boat too!'

Lee was right. She was lucky. Suddenly she could imagine it all cleaned up, and pictured the boathouse bathed in light, with a lovely boat, just like the punt she once been on in

Cambridge. There would be a new wooden jetty. Friends would come round and they would climb into it with a delicious picnic and glide along the Lode. 'It's just like the 'Wind in the Willows,' she said out loud.

'What is?' said Lee.

'This is,' said Jess. 'Have you read the 'Wind in Willows? Ratty and Mole go boating down the river.'

'I can't read,' said Lee, 'but I've seen it on the telly.' *Of course, he can read*, Jess thought. *He's older than me. Everyone my age can read.*

Jess couldn't take it all in. She wanted her Dad to explain it all to her. She wanted him to be there with her, to pick up some of the objects and tell her about them. Where did all this belong in her story? Was granddad like Old Tom and his family? What did Old Tom say they did? Wildfowling, eel catching, poaching, peat digging? Suddenly she felt even closer to Old Tom. He would know, so would Mike.

'Your dad must see this,' Jess said, 'he'll know what everything is.' She looked round for Lee. He was sitting in the bottom of the punt.

'I wonder if it will float,' he said looking at her grinning from grubby ear to grubby ear.

13

THE BOAT HOUSE

Mind how you handle that! That's probably over a hundred years old and the last thing we want is you breaking it.' Jess had never heard Mike sound anxious before, but there was a tone in his voice which made her think that he spent quite a lot of time stopping Lee from breaking things.

'Well what is it? It's a spade of some sort, but why has it got this metal bit sticking out?' Lee held the old spade out towards his father.

'It's a becket. It was a special spade used for cutting out blocks of peat. The metal flange sticking out at right angles to the blade helped the peat digger cut out regular sized and shaped blocks. Do you remember we had a one in the museum just like this, Jess?'

Jess nodded. There were so many old dusty things to look at. Lee was obviously in his element, covered in grime and picking over the old tools and strange objects that were over to one side of the old shed.

'It looks like your granddad – maybe, even great granddad too were peat diggers, Jess. This spade here, with the heart shaped blade and the curve in the metal before it joins the handle, was for slicing away the grass, weeds and top soil, so you could get at the peat. It was called a moor spade.' Mike looked like he could hardly believe his luck.

'Turves were cut from the first week of March to the last week in August. You didn't want frost in it and you wouldn't want to try and dig peat when the land was frozen. In your great granddad's time as many as three hundred men, women and boys were employed every year to produce the turves just in this area of the fen.'

'What did they dig it up for? Was it for putting on gardens?' Jess remembered Jack, their gardener in Nottingham, saying that he had mixed in some peat to help the flowers and vegetables grow.

'The rich, black, peat soil that was uncovered when the fens were drained in the seventeenth century is very good for growing crops, which is why so much food for the rest of the country is grown round here. Because it is like compost, made from rotting vegetation, when it had dried out it could be used as fuel for the cottage fire. There is no coal here in the fens, so turves were the local alternative. They smouldered away in the grate and some cottagers kept their fires alight day and night all year round.'

'In the early days some of the fen men made simple huts out of turf blocks and roofed them with reeds and osiers. Imagine living in a hut like that. It must have been a bit like an igloo.'

'If you got cold, you could always set fire to one of the walls,' said Lee, who seemed not to have been listening.

'What's the boat for?'

'What do you think it is for? There's one like it moored up near Old Tom's. It's flat-bottomed and quite narrow so it can be used on shallow fen drains and the Lodes. This could have been used for carrying turves, for fishing or wildfowling, or simply getting around the fens.'

'Do you think it would still float?' Lee asked, a glint in his eye.

Mike shook his head and smiled. 'Nice idea, but I wouldn't like to try it because the planks have all dried out and I imagine the water would pour in through the cracks.' He paused, thoughtful for a moment, and then said: 'You're very quiet, Jess. Are you sure that your father didn't want to come down with us and look at what is here?'

She looked at the ground and shook her head. She had *so* wanted her dad to come with her, but she knew asking him would be pointless. She wished he was with her now, helping her to take it all in. She was trying to imagine her fen ancestors peat digging, or wild fowling, drifting across the misty fens in that punt. *I will not cry*, she thought.

'There are some bits of old nets over here and some eel griggs. Come and look, Jess. Your very own griggs, all a bit old and battered, but you'll be able to start a museum of your own with all this! I don't want to disturb too much, because I really think your father should see things how they are. I might take a few photos. I'll just go and fetch my camera.'

As he turned to leave the boathouse, he paused to look round as Lee was very quiet somewhere, 'You behave yourself, Lee. I don't want to see you trying to launch the punt while I'm gone. Ok?'

'Ok,' came the reply from Lee who was over in one corner of the shed obviously occupied with something else he had found.

Jess looked through the opening in the shed onto the Lode and the wooden platform. If it was all repaired she would have her own stretch of river, right at the bottom of her garden. If the punt sank, maybe she could have a canoe or little boat and then she could paddle down the Lode and really explore. She imagined herself rowing past Old Tom's, the old man grinning and waving to her while Faithful ran along the bank barking with excitement. 'Right,' came Mike's voice, breaking into her dream. He was back and soon flashing away with his camera at various things in the shed.

'Look what I've found,' Lee called. 'This wooden crate has got old photographs and stuff in it.'

'Let me see,' Mike moved over quickly to where Lee was crouching beside a large wooden crate. 'Careful how you handle things. Some of the glass is broken. These are old. Mind you don't break anything else or cut yourself.'

After a while Mike straightened up and turned to Jess who had moved over to look. 'I think we have found some of your ancestors.'

'I found them,' said Lee.

'All right, I think *Lee* has found some of your ancestors. Come and see.'

Jess stared at a brown coloured photograph in a heavy chipped old frame. The corner of the glass had a crack across it, but through the grime she could make out a young man in a soldier's uniform.

'Looks like the First World War,' Mike said. 'I'd have to

look closer, but that could be the regimental badge of the Cambridgeshire Regiment. Do you know anything about your father's family?'

'Not really, said Jess, 'I remember my grandmother in the old cottage, when I was very little, but my granddad had already died.'

'This could be your great grandfather. We should be able to find out. I might borrow a couple of photos, if that's all right with you, to show Old Tom. He should be able to tell us. I'll take these two and clean them up, so we can have a proper look at them. The rest we'll put back in the box and leave until another day. They've been here a few years now and a few more days won't make much difference. Besides I'd like your dad to be here, as these are personal items.'

14

OLD DIGGER

Yes, that's Old Digger, all right! He must have been about eighteen. He were in the Cambridgeshires along with my old Dad. Look you can see the uniforms are the same.' Old Tom waved a hand at the photograph of his father on the wall. 'Father said that a gang of old boys from the village all went and signed on for the army at the same time. All pals they were and wanted to go in the same regiment and be together when they fought the Ol' Jerry.'

There were about six of them, two of 'em are on the village war memorial, while Dad and Digger were among the lucky ones. One of the others was gassed and never really recovered properly. It was a terrible old war, but then all war is terrible...'

Jess thought the old man was going to add something else, but his voice trailed off. 'Let's see the other one.' Mike had cleaned up the photographs as carefully as he could and he handed the other one over to Old Tom. It was the size of a postcard and the old man had to squint at it, holding it up to the light coming through the cottage door.

'It's my old mate Digger! Young Digger! His father was Old Digger, because he was well-known for his peat digging, so his son, my pal, was known as Young Digger. Look at him! Good looking ol' boy, he was. He must have been about eighteen. There's some writing on the back, can you read it? I don't know where my glasses are.' He handed the photo back to Mike.

'To Alice, with all my love,' it says.

'I thought it might. Alice Bailey was his gal. Good looking she was. Dark hair and flashing eyes. She was quite friendly with my sister, Sarah, although she was a year younger. Oh yes, a lot of the old boys were after Alice.'

Jess tried to imagine someone as old as Old Tom, being young and walking along the bank of the Lode with a girl on his arm. She stroked Faithful's coat and looked out onto the bank of the Lode. It was a glorious August, sunny and hot. Old Tom had been complaining about needing some rain to help everything grow, but from what Jess could see everything was growing and already the harvest was being gathered in from the fields around the village. The harvest flies - horrid little midges that got in your face and hair - were a nuisance, but Jess liked the sun and she wanted these days to go on for ever.

She had already had a trip into Ely to get her new school uniform. There was a bright blue pullover, white shirts, a tie, a blazer with the College badge that her mum had sewn on. Just trying it all on had made her tummy feel a bit funny, and now as she sat quietly enjoying the lush surroundings that she had grown to love, the thought of starting at such a big school when she still knew only a few girls in the village made her feel a bit sick. Faithful must have sensed something, as dogs do, because he looked at her and nuzzled up closer.

'It's alright, boy,' she said burying her face in his soft coat, soothing both the dog and herself.

'Old Digger, he were a rum old boy.' Old Tom's voice cut in to Jess's thoughts and she tuned back in to him. 'Being a peat digger, he liked the lonely life and he had a little hut right out in the fens while he was working on his turf pits. They used to call them turbaries, that was the old name from years and years ago. Some of the turbaries were privately owned and there were some public ones.'

'Old Digger, used to tell us lads all sorts of stories. He would stay out there in his old shelter night after night, all on his own, except he had an old dog with him. Lovely old dog, good ratter. Unlike that soft ol' thing, run a mile from a rat, I should think.'

If he's talking about you, thought Jess, as Faithful had begun to look up at the sound of his master's voice, *I bet you're as good as any dog. Take no notice.*

'What sort of stories?' It was Mike's voice.

'Smuggling, for one. There were some rum ol' boys about. And the Fens were dangerous anyway. You wouldn't go out at night unless there was a good moon and a lot of the ol' boys carried a safe-keep with them. Old Digger always had a little box in his pocket. Digger told me, his father had once shown him what was inside and said to him, just as he had reached out to touch what looked like bits of curled wood or something, 'them's nail clippings of a dead women, best safe-keep of all.'

Some old boys carried around a verse of the bible written

on a piece of paper and put in a nut shell. Anything would do, really, as long as they believed in it.'

'Like my grandfather and Old Digger, those ol' boys didn't bother much about who owned the land or water. They believed that the birds and the fish belonged to everybody.'

'They used to set up nets on poles as traps for lapwings and peewits. Sometimes they would have a live decoy pegged out with it. When the birds settled they'd pull on a line and the poles would collapse and the nets would trap the birds.'

'It weren't no sport, you know. It was all done so as they could, feed themselves and their families. They'd barter goods and trade with one another. That was a good system, that one. If you had too much of something and someone else had something you wanted you could do a bit of business without needing money in your pocket.

'Many of the old 'uns suffered from the ague. They tell us now it was a sort of malaria, brought on by being bitten by all the mosquitoes in the Fens. They used to dose 'emselves up with poppy head tea or laudanum to take away the shivers and shakes.'

'If that weren't bad enough many of the old 'uns were crippled up with 'the screws', the rheumatics, which weren't so surprising considering how wet the old fens were and how their old cottages were so damp an' all. I've been lucky really, a few aches and pains in my knees. I went to see a doctor once and he said, 'What do you expect at your age, my man?' So I thought, if that's all there is to doctoring, I'll look after myself. A little drop of whisky is my medicine.

'There were millions of mozzies, 'specially when it got round evening time. If you were out on a boat and coming home that time them davils would bite you to pieces. Some of the old boys would hang a piece of net from their caps so it would cover their faces. All the men wore something on their heads, just like the women wore the old fen bonnets that covered the back of the neck, and sheltered the sides of the face from the sun and the insects. Then there were the fen blows when the old soil would blow across the flat fields like a sand storm and those bonnets would keep the dirt out of their face and hair. Very practical they were.'

'It was because of the mosquitoes that the peat diggers used to start the working day at six in the morning and finish at three in the afternoon, before the mozzies got busy. That piece of net could be dampened to keep them a bit cool, or they could put sprigs of plants in it to keep the flies off and it would help keep the mozzies at bay.'

'Have you ever drunk paigle tea?' Old Tom said, looking up at Mike with a smile.

'I thought you were going to say poppy head tea, for a moment,' said Mike. 'No, I've never had paigle tea or poppy-head tea for that matter.'

'We used to drink it. There were a lot of cowslips in them days, you don't see so many now. You could also make cowslip wine, along with elderberry wine. That could be some strong stuff an all.'

'By the time I were growing up between the wars, the old ways were already going. Then with the Second World War and the 'War Ag', whole parts of the fen, like Adventurers Fen between here and Burwell, were drained for food production. After that it was mainly about farming, and the fields grew bigger and the machines come in, all to feed the growing population. With all the machines, there weren't as much work for the old agricultural labourers so they went off to find work in the towns, I suppose.

'Yes, I've seen a lot of change. Some of it for the better, but I miss the old ways. They reckon they're going to bring back more of the old Fen. I shan't live to see it. It won't be the same, shouldn't think they'll allow any punt gunners on there or eel fishermen, unless it's all pretend for the visitors. I don't suppose they'll ever know how hard it really was for us out here. Probably just as well, I wouldn't wish it on 'em.'

15

YOUNG DIGGER

Jess celebrated her eleventh birthday. It wasn't a huge celebration. Jess knew that they didn't have much money. There were some cards and a cake.

Mike called round with Lee and they brought Lee's younger sister, Cassie. Cassie was quite small and not at all like Lee. She was about a year younger than Jess, but quite confident. 'Someone told us that it was your birthday,' Mike said. They'd brought her some presents and another card.

Lee began to devour a large slice of cake. 'Happy Birthday, lovely cake.'

'Don't drop crumbs all over the place, sorry about this,' said Mike.

'It's all right,' her mum said. 'You enjoy it. That's what cake is for.'

'Come on, open your presents,' Lee said, through a mouthful of icing and crumbs.

Jess opened the presents. One was a book and the other was some pretty hair bands and a lovely scarf, the sort that Cassie wore. 'Thank you,' she said, feeling quite emotional.

'I thought you might like this.' Mike said to Jess. It was a CD that had been produced by the Museum. It contained songs by John and some of Mike's stories. 'The songs are good, not so sure about the stories. I won't listen to it myself.'

'Thank you,' Jess said. 'I'll listen to it later.'

Jess took a big piece of cake round for Old Tom and then took Faithful for a walk along the Lode bank. Lee and Cassie joined her, while Mike stopped to talk to Old Tom. When they got back to Old Tom's cottage, they went through to the garden and began picking the ripe plums.

When Jess had picked enough she made her way back to her place by the front door. She could hear Old Tom talking to Mike. He seemed to want to tell him his whole life story. She didn't mean to listen, but it was always so interesting.

'Young Digger were a real ol' fen boy. He had black hair and skin that browned easy, like his father. He were stocky, smaller than me, but tough.

'We was always in trouble at school. We had to walk up the school and back home again at lunch times if we wanted a bit of dockey. We'd get to playing and messing about, sometimes we would be rolling marbles along the road or kicking an old ball along. There were hardly any vehicles on the roads then. You'd get some horse and carts or donkey carts, that's about all.'

'Of course, we used to dawdle along eating an apple or something we pulled off someone's tree as we went past. Then we'd look up and there'd be old Walling, the schoolmaster, at the school gate with his cane in his hand.'

"'You're late," he'd say, and we'd get a crack across the backside or the hand with the old stick. Good way to start school! No wonder we couldn't wait to leave. Still we learnt right from wrong and how to read and write a bit. Mind you I don't think I saw Digger ever write more than his name when he had to. What did we need to write much for anyway? Mostly everyone we knew lived round here, so we could talk to them.'

Jess had filled a bag with ripe plums from the garden, to take home, so her mother could make a pie, but sitting there in the sun with Old Tom talking in the background she couldn't resist tucking into them and enjoying the feeling of the sweet juice running down her chin.

She felt as if she had been in Fens End for years. It was getting towards the end of August and the first day at the new school was looming even closer. 'It's the plums making my tummy twitch, Faithful,' she said out loud to her companion, who had settled beside her to enjoy the sunshine. 'Not school, I'm not worried about it. Honestly!' she said to the dog, who was looking up at her. She wasn't sure Faithful believed her, or she believed it herself. *At least they don't use the cane anymore*, she thought.

'We both left school when we was fourteen.' Old Tom had settled into his story. Mike was listening with his notebook on his lap. 'Men we were then, none of this teenager business they have today. In our day you were either a boy at school or a man out to work. Nothing in between. That was the same year Edward the Seventh abdicated so he could marry that Mrs Simpson.'

'The next year there was a party on the village green to celebrate the Coronation. There was a local dance band that played and we all tried to get a young lady on our arm. After all, we were fifteen years old and had a bob or two in our pockets.' Old Tom rubbed his hands together and chuckled at the memory.

'Anyway dad got himself a job with the Great Ouse River Board and said he'd try and get me a job there, but I got a job at the Old Hall working on the estate. The most useful thing I did was learn to drive a tractor. By the time I were seventeen I could drive an old lorry and take crops and animals to market. During the winter I used to take loads of sugar beet to the factory at Queen Adelaide near Ely. Digger got a job there a couple of times when they were taking on extra men for the beet season. They called it 'the campaign'.'

'All the talk those years was of another war. My poor old mother was worried I would have to go. Father, of course, knew what war was and couldn't believe it was going to happen again. "We fought the war that was supposed to end all wars and 'ere we are about to start again twenty years after," he used to say. "But, whatever happens, we have to stand up to that ol' Hitler."'

'He reckoned it would be different from the last war when they were stuck in the trenches for months on end. "Now they've got tanks and planes. No one will be safe from bombing." We were all issued with gas masks.'

'Soon after war was declared, Old Digger and father both joined the Local Defence Volunteers. They used to meet up the pub at the top of the Lane. He armed himself with his old shotgun and he was issued with an arm band.'

'We used to see 'em drilling up and down the road, about twenty ol' boys, armed with anything from pitch forks to shot guns. Digger used to laugh and say: "Well we can all sleep better in our beds now, knowing if the old Germans do come, they won't get past that lot".'

'There was work to be had during the first part of the war, when nothing seemed to be happening. They were building a hospital for the RAF at Ely and there were airfields being built all round the area. We all knew that if the war wasn't over soon, we'd have to go and do our bit.

'We talked about joining the Cambridgeshire Regiment, which were Territorials, but Digger had fallen for a girl and so we carried on working. Being involved in food production we were doing essential war work. Just as well we didn't sign up to anything. Them poor fellers shipped out to the Far East in 1941, arrived at Singapore, then just a week or two after they was over run by the Japanese and had to surrender. They suffered terrible on that Death Railway. I reckon I had a lucky escape from that.

'You said Digger had fallen for a girl. This was Alice was it?'

'Alice Bailey, yes. She were a lovely little ol' gal. Trouble was...' Jess was listening and in the pause she sensed the old man reaching for the bottle of whisky and pouring some into his tumbler, then lighting up one of his roll ups. 'Trouble was, so had I. I don't think he ever found out. If he had I'm sure we would have fallen out.'

'I used to hang around when I knew she might be coming along. I'd say "Hello" and that, but I was terrible shy with girls. I always got all tongue tied. Digger used to take her to the pictures over in Soham. I didn't think she really took much notice of me at all.'

'Early in 1941 we both got invitations from the government to do our bit for King and Country. Some old boys tried to avoid it, but I thought if I went off and became a hero, then maybe Alice might notice me.'

'Because I could drive, I suppose, I was sent to the Royal Army Service Corps. Our job was to keep supplies moving for the troops in the front line. Digger was in the Parachute Regiment. My plans to impress Alice hadn't exactly worked out.'

'I trained all over the place. In 1944 we were training for going back to mainland Europe. It was all very hush, hush, as they used to say.'

'I got a few days embarkation leave in the Spring of 1944 and came back here. It seemed strange. Not much had changed really. There was a lot of farming activity with the War Ag and that. Mother and father were pleased to see me, but a lot of my mates were away.

I admit I was a bit frightened and sat there by the old Lode here wondering if I would see it all again. Planes were flying backwards and forwards. This whole area was like an aircraft carrier.'

'The Yanks were about and I met the young flier who was going out with my sister. He brought me a nice bottle of rye whiskey and some big ol' cigars. I hadn't smoked many cigars and the first one I tried, boy, did that make me cough! I thought I was going to throw up.'

'On the last day of the leave, I was sitting along the bank there when Alice comes along. She sits down beside me and starts talking away. She'd seen Digger when he had some days leave and she said they'd talked about getting married after the war. She said she'd wait and see. She said the war did strange things to people. She told me that she had become very friendly with a young American airman who had been stationed over Bury St Edmunds way. She'd gone to some dance or other with my sister Sarah and met him there. She said he was a lovely young man and they'd seen each other as much as possible for several weeks. She said he'd told her he would take her back to the States with him once the war was over.'

'It was Sarah's feller who came round and found her a few days later to tell her. Her young man's plane had gone down over Germany on a raid. All the crew were lost. She said that was the end of her dreams.'

'We kept talking and, it was getting dark, but it was still a warm evening. I don't know how it all happened. I suppose it was the war and young people finding comfort with each other. I told her that I'd always really liked her and she said she knew all along. I told her I was going back the next day. Well one thing led to another.'

There was a long silence. Mike seemed to know what Old Tom was talking about, which was more than Jess did. She got up and went out onto the tow path. Faithful trotted along beside her. The sun was beginning to sink down in the sky and the light was reflecting off the Lode. Faithful kept dashing off into the reeds and undergrowth and coming back looking very pleased wagging his tail.

Jess was trying to imagine Old Tom as a young man with Alice saying goodbye along this bank, neither knowing whether they would see each other again. War was an awful thing. She wondered what happened to Digger. And why was his photo in her old boathouse?

I need to get my dad talking again, maybe he can answer some of these questions, she thought as she headed home for Lavender Cottage that evening.

16

CASUALTIES OF WAR

The last day of the school holiday was a lovely September day. Jess thought it might not seem so bad going back to school if the weather wasn't so lovely.

Charlotte, one of her new friends from the village school had been round to see a few times with Holly Bailey. 'We don't see much of you up in the village,' Charlotte had said.

'No,' said Jess, 'We've got a lot to do here on the cottage, so I've been helping my mum.' Jess didn't think she would talk about Old Tom and Faithful and the cottage. She felt it was something to keep for herself as long as she could.

Mike had brought Lee and Cassie over again. They were all in Old Tom's garden picking fruit. They had picked bags full of ripe plums and now they were gathering up some apples. Lee was helping by sitting amongst the branches of one of the plum trees, dropping plums with unerring accuracy on his sister, who was squealing and running away to complain to anyone who would listen.

Perhaps, Jess thought, *there was something to be said for being an only child*. It was fun having someone to play with though. Things at Lavender Cottage were still not very good. Her dad wouldn't take an interest in anything and her mother still looked worried to death about him. Jess had tried to talk to him, but it was no use. Her friends took her mind off things a bit.

The hedges at the side of the long garden were bursting with blackberries and Jess was trying to pick them and eat them without getting tangled up or torn to pieces by the brambles. She surprised herself. A few months ago she would never have dreamed of eating fruit like this without washing it.

Cassie joined her by the hedge and from somewhere behind them she could hear an ominous cracking sound as Lee came down from the tree rather suddenly. 'Help!' came a cry from somewhere in the grass at the foot of the tree. 'Come and help me.'

Jess turned to go. 'He's all right,' said Cassie, 'He's always doing things like this. He will say he's broken something and then the next minute he'll be up and running around again.'

Jess tried to ignore Lee's yelps, as Cassie seemed to be, but he kept calling and eventually Jess went over to him. 'About time,' he said from where he was lying still clutching a piece of broken branch with a few plums attached. 'Didn't you hear me calling? The branch broke and I've hurt my ankle.'

'Let me help you up,' said Jess. As she began to pull Lee to his feet he yelped and hopped. 'Can you walk on it?'

'I don't think so, it really hurts.'

'We'd better get you over to the cottage where your dad can have a look at it.' Jess began to steer Lee towards the cottage. He clung on to her and hopped and winced. As they got near to the cottage, Jess could hear Old Tom talking.

'You see, I've seen the Ol' Dog again. I was by the front door taking the evening air and he come along the bank. He were looking for me. He just stood there on the tow path, staring with those big eyes. I haven't got long and that's why I really need your help.'

'Sit here,' Jess said to Lee, helping him to an old bench that stood by the back door, 'I'll get your father.' As she entered the cottage the two men stopped talking and looked towards her.

'It's the little ol' gal,' Tom said. 'Now have you picked a good lot of fruit to take home? Pity to see it all go to waste.'

'Yes, we've picked quite a lot, but Lee's hurt his ankle. He's just by the back door.'

Mike got up to go to him. 'Won't be a minute. I'm afraid my son is rather accident prone.'

'You can fetch me a few ripe plums in if you like. I enjoy a bit of fresh fruit. Always have done and there in't no fresher than what you can pick from your own trees and bushes. Are you back at school yet?'

'Not yet, I start at Soham Village College tomorrow.'

'How old are you then?'

'Eleven. Remember, we had some cake?'

'Oh yes, I remember the cake, very nice too, thank you. Eleven are you? Do you like school? I couldn't wait until I was fourteen to leave and go out to work. Mind you my mother and father both left school at twelve. How about that? I suppose children today are much luckier than we were. I mean you can stay on and learn languages and everything. Bonjour, au revoir, gutten tag, auf wiedersehn, that's about all I learnt.'

'At school?'

'No during the war when I was in France and Germany.'

'You were going to tell me something about that,' Mike said as he entered the room. 'Lee'll be all right, the usual maximum amount of fuss over a minor injury. But I've told him, if it isn't better by tomorrow I'll take him to get it checked out. He's well known up the Minor Injuries Clinic. He's sitting out there, go and feed him some plums or an apple or something, Jess. That should keep him quiet for a while. Cassie's still picking away, but she'll make so much fuss, I doubt whether she'll have anything to show for it.'

Jess went into the garden and collected some plums and apples and joined Lee on the bench. Cassie was running around in the field with Faithful, who was making the most of having. someone else to make a fuss of him. She could hear Old Tom and Mike talking through the open door.

'...our job was to follow them and keep them supplied. We also had ambulances with us for the wounded. Royal Army Service Corps, it don't sound very glamorous and it wasn't. But the fighting men had to have supplies. We followed the 11th Armoured Division across Europe after D-Day.'

'Young Digger copped it a few days after the landing. His lot parachuted in, but they landed all over the place and had to fight their way out to rejoin their pals.'

'Young Digger was killed?'

'No, he weren't killed. He was very seriously wounded,

after a spell in hospital over there, he was shipped back to England. Of course, I didn't know any of this at the time.'

'We pushed on. The 11th made one of the fastest drives into enemy territory in the whole war. They captured Antwerp and went through the German held parts of the Netherlands. We crossed the Rhine in the March of 1945. There was some heavy fighting, I tell you. The Germans were good soldiers and they weren't going to give up easily.'

Lee seemed to have recovered from his injuries sufficiently to limp off towards the hen house from which he soon appeared carrying a mildly protesting hen in his hands. He set off round the garden after Cassie. *Good*, thought Jess, *I want to hear what they are talking about without Lee fidgeting around.* She knew it wasn't his fault. Mike had told her all about Lee's ADHD and how he was dyslexic and so found it really difficult to read.

'15th April, 1945. Mean anything to you?' Old Tom's voice sounded strange. Jess wasn't sure if he was angry or sad.

'No, can't say it does,' Mike answered after a few moments.

'It's a date, I shall never forget. That was the day the Division entered Bergen-Belsen. The Germans had agreed to surrender it peacefully. The war was nearly over, the Americans were pushing forward along with us and the Russians were closing in from the other side. You know what Bergen-Belsen was, you being a historian and all that?'

'Oh yes,' Jess heard Mike's voice, 'I'm afraid I do know what Bergen-Belsen was. And you were there?'

'Bergen-Belsen?' Jess strained to hear every word. She knew the name as well. She had done a project at school.

It was where Anne Frank died.

'Nothing could have prepared us for what we saw there. It haunts me to this day. I was told there were some 60,000 prisoners in that concentration camp. They were living skeletons. The men wore a sort of striped pyjamas and the women had striped flannel gowns, a bit like night dresses. Some were in rags, no shoes or anything.'

'We took food supplies there. There was an Ely man there driving an ambulance. You probably knew him, Percy Burrows, had the newsagents in the High Street. It was still there last time I went to Ely.'

'Yes, it's still there. I know the family.'

'Well he was there, I saw him. But he never talked about it afterwards. None of us did. Not for years. Thirteen thousand corpses had to be buried. We made the German guards do that, at first, but then we had to use bulldozers because it was such a huge job.'

'Even after we got there, them poor souls was dying at the rate of a hundred or more a day. The place was filthy and disease ridden. It stank. The smell...the smell was foul, got right in your pores. You felt you could never scrub yourself clean of it.'

'Some of the men with us were married and had families at home. I think it were worse for them, seeing all the children dead and dying. We'd all seen terrible things before, of course. Tanks blown up, men on fire. We'd all lost pals. But this...we'd never seen nothing like that before. Nothing had prepared us for that. Nothing could have prepared us.'

Jess heard some whisky being poured and there was a pause.

'Just imagine, I'd never been out of the Fens and here I was in the middle of Germany! The war was over but I didn't come back straightaway. I'd thought a lot about Alice since I'd left over a year before. I'd had a letter from my mother at Christmas time 1944 telling me my old pal Digger had come home wounded. She also told me that he had married Alice. Now my mother, bless her, could have a bit of a disapproving side to her and she informed me that they had a baby boy, already.'

'I had been thinking in all those early days after D-Day when we'd been coming through France and into Holland, that if I came through the War, I might go home to Alice. I mean she seemed fond of me and I was certainly fond of her. I imagined us getting a little cottage and setting up home. You know, we'd have a couple of kids, a boy who took after me and a little girl like her. I suppose I wasn't the only one out there who had dreams like that to keep them going. I mean, you needed something to look forward to, didn't you?' There was another long pause, Jess could feel the sadness in that small room. 'But now she had gone and married Digger, that wasn't going to happen. So I got on with the soldiering.'

'There was a lot of work to do out there and somehow, I suppose, I thought if I kept busy, I wouldn't have to face up to coming home and starting again. Then I got another letter from my mother saying that Sarah had married her young American flier and gone off to the States and when would I be coming home?'

17

HOMECOMING

I arrived home in the March of 1946. I was pleased to see the old fen again and mother and father were pleased to see me. But I couldn't settle. I'd wake up with nightmares of what I'd seen. I took myself off for hours at a time down the Lode or across on Monks Fen, just to get way from everyone, I suppose.'

'I took the old punt out and spent hours just fishing. I wasn't really bothered whether I caught anything. I was just sitting there, staring at the water. Today they probably have a name for it...'

'Post traumatic stress disorder,' Mike said.

'Thass the one. We didn't have none of that then! You were given a new suit, a railway pass and sent home to get on with your life. I got off the train at Soham, they had a station there in them days and I walked across the fields home. Of course, as I said, mother and father were pleased to see me. And our old dog! But I were in a bit of a state, to tell the truth.

'There had been some changes. Alan Bloom, you've heard of him? He was a real character. He drained a large part of Adventurer's Fen for the War Ag. I know it was important to grow as much food as we could, but Father didn't like to see the old fen go. He said to me, "It's all going, son. All the old ways. Soon there won't be any peat digging, wildfowling, nothing. It'll all be about growing food. It'll be like America with great areas of corn and other crops. It'll all be done by machines." He were right, weren't he? He was just an ignorant old fen boy, but he could see what was happening.'

'How you were supposed to just pick up the pieces, I don't know? It weren't easy. There were local men who'd been with the Cambridgeshires who'd been captured at Singapore and had to work on the Death Railway. Them that survived came home like living skeletons. They didn't get any special help and they suffered terrible. They were just expected to get on with their lives and most of them did an' all. Me, I didn't really want to talk to anyone or see anyone. Anytime I saw any earth moving machines, I kept seeing them poor creatures tumbling into a pit. It kept me awake at night.'

'It's a serious form of depression, I suppose.' It was Mike again. 'Brought about by what you'd been through. People who've lost a loved one or lost their job, or something like that, can experience something similar, I think. The mind can't cope, so they sort of shut down.'

Of course, Jess thought. *That's it, that's what has happened to Daddy. He lost his business and had to sell everything and move down here. All those people who lost their jobs. It was all too much for him and he shut down.*

He has depression. Jess felt a huge sense of relief. Her daddy was ill and the illness had a name. *If he was ill, he could be made better! He would come back!*

'Lee, put it down. She doesn't want to be carried around.' Cassie's voice cut through Jess's thoughts. Lee was heading in her direction still carrying the old hen, but Cassie was doing the clucking. Lee turned and let the hen free tossing her in the direction of Cassie, who shrieked and ran away.

Lee disappeared into the little hen house and emerged carrying a fresh egg in each hand. 'Fancy something to eat?' he said to Jess with a big grin.   Jess loved coming over to Old Tom's and collecting the eggs. He had taught her how to feel for eggs, gently moving her hand underneath the chicken's body, feeling the soft, velvety feathers and the prickly straw and then, finally the smooth warm shell of an egg.

'She won't bite you. Go on,' Old Tom had chuckled when she hesitated thinking the hen was going to peck her. 'We'll make a country girl of you yet.'

'Now you must have that one for your breakfast,' he had said. And she had. She boiled it for breakfast the next day and ate it with toast soldiers. Egg and toast had never tasted better.

She was a little worried that Lee might suddenly throw his eggs at her and just smash them, but he didn't. He put them down carefully on the bench and said: 'They're mine. Look after them. I don't want Cassie taking them.' Then he was off whooping up the garden scattering chickens in his path.

In the silence that followed Lee's departure, Jess could hear Tom's voice from inside. 'I was up the Lode, right up near where it joins the main river. That was one of my favourite little spots, I loved the view right across the fen. I allus thought of it as Alice and my meeting place. There weren't many people about and I could just lay there on the grass for hours. It was early Summer. I was miles away in thought, when I heard this child's voice. I looked round and there was a little lad. He was toddling along, falling over, laughing, getting up again. Lovely looking little lad. And there was Alice.'

'She looked older, more tired, than when I last saw her. She caught the little boy's hand and held onto him. I just looked at her, I didn't know what to say for a moment.'

' "I heard you was back," she said. "Hadn't seen you, wondered if you might be here. Thought you might have come and seen Digger."'

' "Yes," I said, "I heard you and him got married. I'm sorry I haven't been round. I haven't really wanted to see anyone. How is he?" '

' "He's…" she stared out across the fen and pulled the little lad a bit closer to her. " You know he got wounded in Normandy?" '

' "I did hear something. I was told it was pretty serious".'

' "Yes, he was caught by a shell blast. Bits of the shell went into his body. When he got back here, he was doing really quite well and seemed on the mend".'

' "You got married?" '

' "I was expecting a baby and you know what this village is like. The old tongues were wagging, your mother's among them. Digger and I were courting before he went to France. He'd always said we would marry when he came home a hero. He came home a hero and we got married." '

' "Smashing little ol' boy you've got there." I says. "So everything's worked out as you hoped then?" She didn't say nothing for a while. "You haven't been to see him", she says.'

' "No. But I will do, now I've seen you and the little feller here. I've just been keeping out of everybody's way that's all." '

' "He'd like to see you." she says, "He'd like to see anything." She just looked at me, with this strange, sad expression on her face, and then she suddenly blurted out: "He's blind, Tom. Digger is blind! There was a piece of shrapnel lodged in his head that the surgeons couldn't get at. It must have moved or something because he began to lose his sight and now he can barely see anything just shapes and shadows".'

'"Alice, I'm sorry," I said, "I had no idea." I hadn't either. I sat there on that riverbank, thinking I was the only one with any problems in the world and my old mate was going blind and I didn't know.'

Jess suddenly felt that she shouldn't be listening. It was like spying. Her mother said that you never hear good things if you listened to other people's conversations when you shouldn't. She got up and went down the garden to see what Lee and Cassie were up to. It must be getting late and she ought to be getting home. She started the College tomorrow. The holiday was over.

'I've got to go now,' she called out to Lee and Cassie, who for once weren't fighting but sitting in the long grass eating some plums.

'We'll probably be going as soon as Dad has finished talking. Do you start at school tomorrow as well?'

'Yes.'

'I hate school,' said Lee.

'Actually, I quite like it,' said Cassie. 'I get a chance to see my friends and we'll be doing a play this term and I want to get a part in it.'

'You *would* like it,' said Lee. 'Ooh, *please Miss*, can I carry your books, it's so lovely to be back at school. Please give me lots of work to do.'

'Oh, shut up, Lee.'

'No, you're a geek!' And with that he threw a plum with his usual accuracy. It splattered against Cassie's forehead. She let out a howl and Jess thought it really was time to leave.

'Bye,' she said. 'It really is time to go.'

As Jess went through the cottage, she handed some of the plums she had picked to Old Tom. 'I've got to go home now. I've got school, tomorrow.'

'Thank you for these. You take care then, and you come round any time you like, you're always welcome. You can take Faithful for a walk next time.' The dog looked up at her from where he was lying by his master's feet as if to say, 'I'll keep you to that.'

'I'd like that,' she said. 'Bye, Bye, Mike.'

'Oh, Jess, I forgot to give you these. I took a copy because they are such nice photographs.' He handed her the photographs that they had found in the boathouse.

When she got out of the cottage, she stopped on the towpath to look at the photographs again. There was Old Digger standing proud in his army uniform and Young Digger, wearing a suit, 'all dressed up in his Sunday best' as her mum would say. Her mind was racing: could these two men in these faded photographs really be her great grandfather and grandfather? She must ask her dad.

The sun was beginning to sink in the sky as she headed for Lavender Cottage. She could hear Faithful coming along behind her. *He doesn't usually follow me*, she thought as she turned to send him back to Old Tom's.

But it wasn't Faithful. It was a big, black dog. The head was level with her face. The eyes were huge, like saucers.

Normally Jess would have been terrified by a dog of this size, on the loose with no owner in sight, but she wasn't afraid. She looked at the dog and the dog looked at her. It wasn't fierce or growling. It was just looking at her sadly.

Then the dog turned and padded back along the tow path towards the burning red glow of the setting sun.

18

THE BIG SCHOOL

Jess struggled with her tie. She couldn't leave it until tomorrow morning to get it right and when she had asked her mum for help, she got the usual mum response: 'You should have learnt to do it sooner. Fancy leaving everything until the last moment!'

'I've never worn a tie,' Jess said hopelessly, which simply drew the other usual mum response: 'Ask your father.'

He was sitting in his usual chair, with the daily newspaper on his lap. She wasn't sure whether he was reading it or not. The television was flickering away in the corner, but he wasn't really watching. The photographs she had brought home from Old Tom's were still on the small table beside him. The only difference was that the plums from Old Tom's had all gone and in their place was a small pile of stones.

'Dad, Dad, can you help me with this, please?' She held out the striped tie towards him.

He looked up at her, as if he had never seen her before. 'I've just had some plums,' he said. 'Reminded me of...

what's the problem?'

'I don't know how to tie a tie.'

'What do you need to tie one for anyway? You're a girl.'

'School uniform, Dad.'

'You look very smart,' he said. 'Are you going somewhere?'

'Yes, Dad, I'm going to the College, tomorrow.'

'Tomorrow? You start school again tomorrow? Where have those weeks gone?' He was shaking his head and looked confused. 'Have you had a good holiday?' He looked at her, blinking, as though dazzled by light. 'We didn't go anywhere did we?'

'We came here, dad.' Jess spoke slowly, aware that this was the first time he had really spoken to her for weeks.

'I suppose we did,' he smiled wearily. 'Do you like it?'

'I love it, dad,' she said. 'It's the best place ever!' As she said it, Jess realised that she really meant it. She didn't miss Nottingham at all. He smiled again, slowly looking around the room as if he was seeing it for the first time.

'I'm glad. I was worried that you might not like it... those plums,' he said, losing his train of thought. 'They reminded me of...' he trailed off again. 'Now what's all this about a tie?' He said it so suddenly that Jess almost jumped.

'I have to wear a tie for school.'

'Right,' her father said. 'Let's see now...'

Jess followed his instructions and then turned to look at herself in the mirror over the fireplace. The tie seemed to look the way it should.

'I think I've done it,' she gasped, smiling broadly as she spun round to show her dad.

'Not bad at all. Let's have a look at you.'

She stood in front of her dad. For the first time in weeks,

almost since the day they had arrived in Lavender Cottage, three or four months ago, he was looking at her properly. 'You're taller,' he said. 'You're so...so grown up.' He moved a strand of hair across her face and tucked it behind her ear. He just stared at her for a moment, before saying: 'So this is what you are wearing for what?'

'The College, Dad. I start tomorrow.'

'You'll enjoy that,' he said. 'I went to Soham Grammar School. We had to pass the eleven-plus in those days. It was all boys there from all over, Ely, Littleport, even Cambridge.'

'My little girl,' he said, and she could see a tear beginning to trickle down his unshaven cheek. 'My little girl, getting all grown up, going to my old school. Let me look at you again.' He pushed her, gently, a little further away.

My Dad is coming back to me, she thought. He had said more to her in the last few minutes than he had in all the weeks since they had moved into Lavender Cottage. *It was like when Old Tom was feeling so sad after the war and then he saw Alice and her little boy, and it woke him up.*

'Where have the years gone?' he said. 'Doesn't seem long since you were just a little baby. And now look at you, going off to the big school. You'll enjoy it and make lots of friends.'

'I enjoyed those plums.' He said suddenly. 'They tasted just like plums used to taste when I was young. There was a fellow lived along the Lode bank. He was a friend of my mother and father. I suppose he was a bit like an uncle to me. I used to go round there a lot when I was your age. He had an orchard and there were gooseberries, plums, apples. We had quite a few in our garden, but his somehow, well, his just seemed *better*'. He was smiling at the memory and it was the first real smile Jess had seen for a very long time. She wanted to call her mum, so that she could see it too, but she was afraid to break the spell. And her mind was racing: *I think he means Old Tom! My dad knows Old Tom!*

'He was very kind to me. He used to take me fishing and tell me about the Fens all round here. He taught me to skate.'

'What about your father?' Jess asked tentatively, already knowing the answer. 'Didn't he take you fishing or skating?'

'He couldn't,' she saw him hesitate and then she saw the tears begin to fill his eyes… 'Haven't I ever told you? He lost his sight. He was wounded during the war and by the time I was growing up he was blind.'

Jess took a deep breath, picked up one of the old photographs she had tucked into her blazer pocket and handed it to her father. 'Dad, do you know who this is?'

'Where did you get this, Jess?' He stared at the photograph and Jess could see a tear trickle down his cheek. She wanted to wipe it away. She wasn't sure if he was happy or sad – perhaps she had made him worse? But he was smiling.

'Oh Jess, this is my dad! Your granddad!' he looked from Jess to the photograph several times. 'My goodness, yes, that's him! He peered closely to get a better look. 'He's really quite young in this photo. I remember seeing it before. Jess! Wherever did you find it? That's Robert Barnes, my father.'

'Robert?'

'Well, that was his proper name, but no one ever called him that. Anyone who came to the house called him…'

Digger! Jess almost said it out loud, thoughts racing through her mind.

'Digger! He was called Digger. His father was William Barnes, quite a character by all accounts, known as Digger. When my dad was born he became known as 'Young Digger.'

'And Grandma?' Jess was almost too afraid to ask.

'Alice. Alice Bailey. In a small village like this there weren't that many families and everyone tended to know each other or be related. There must be a photograph of her somewhere.'

Jess's head was in a spin. So many thoughts came crowding in as she thought of all the stories Old Tom had told to Mike. She shouldn't have been listening, but she had heard them.

My grandfather was old Tom's best friend? There were so many questions she wanted to ask her dad, but she knew it was too soon. The most important thing was that in the last few minutes, he was like dad again. She felt she was like Bobby in 'The Railway Children' when her dad came back to her.

'Where did you get the photograph?' he asked.

She was about to answer, when her mum appeared in the doorway. 'Come on, love, you must get to bed, you've got an early start in the morning. Big day tomorrow, going up to the College.'

'It's all right, love,' her dad said. 'Jess and I have been talking about our roots. She's got a lot to learn, but it can wait. A good night's sleep is what you need young lady. We have plenty of time to talk when you are not at school. Give us a kiss, and then off you go.'

Her mum stood in the doorway, looking quizzically from one to the other.

'It's all right, love, it really is. I've...had some plums!' He laughed. 'No, I'm all right. It's all right. Believe me.'

Jess kissed her dad. He put his arms round her. His face was all rough and stubbly with quite a beard, but it was the best hug she had ever had. He had things to tell her. *Just wait until you hear some of the things I know,* she thought. But for now, they could wait.

As she turned to say goodnight to her mum, she saw tears rolling down her face. 'It's all right, Mum,' she said: 'Don't worry about me, I'll be fine.' She gave her mum a kiss and skipped up the stairs to her snug little bedroom under the thatch.

'Jessica Barnes, sit up straight and pay attention!' Mike was her teacher. But how could she pay attention when that big old Black Dog was looking through the window. But it was all right because her dad was in the school and he was taking care of her and...

It was a relief when Mr Cock-a Doodle-Doo woke her from her fitful sleep. She knew she could enjoy just a few more minutes dozing in bed before she had to get up. Her tummy did a little flip.

'Oh, Tedder,' she said hugging him tight. 'I'm off to big school today. But I don't mind, Dad will be here when I get home.'

19

BACK TO OUR ROOTS

Better still, her Dad walked her along to the bus stop in the morning. She felt nervous, but there were several of her class mates, all in their new uniforms, gathering to wait for the bus.

'All right, Jess?' It was Charlotte. 'Did you have a good holiday? Didn't see you around much. Mind you we went to Skegness for two weeks.'

'I'll leave you with your friends,' her dad said. He was up early and had shaved, Jess noticed. He'd even put on the aftershave she had bought for him last Christmas. She gave him a hug.

'Have a good day,' he said. 'Enjoy yourself. I'll meet you here at 3. 30.'

'Is that your granddad?' Charlotte asked as her dad wandered off towards Lode Lane.

By the time Jess stepped off the bus at the end of her first day at the College, her head was bursting with new information and her school bag was crammed full of new books, timetables and letters. The College was certainly very big and she felt very little.

At Break, a big boy had come over to her small group of Year Sevens as they ate their sandwiches. 'All right, Charley,' he had said. 'If you get any bother from anyone, just tell me and I'll sort it.' With that he cracked his knuckles and strolled off with a group of equally big boys.

'My brother, Matt,' Charlotte said. 'The big banana. Thinks he's cool. He promised Mum he'd keep an eye on me. S'pect he'll do the same for you.'

The teachers all seemed kind and everyone was helpful, but it was so different from just having Miss Matthews and moving around such a big school was tiring and confusing. As the school bus returned to the village that evening and the older children pushed their way off, she was relieved that she had survived the first day. She was even more pleased to see her dad standing there waiting for her.

'Your granddad's come to meet you,' Charlotte said.

'He's my dad,' Jess said.

'Oh,' said Charlotte, 'he looks as old as my granddad.'

'He probably is,' said Jess, 'But he's my dad.'

'How did you get on?' her dad asked.

Jess could see the anxiety in his eyes. 'Fine, it was fine. Honestly!'

He put out his hand and it was the nicest feeling in the world when she held up hers and his big hand wrapped up her little one.

'I went to have a look at our garden while you were at school. There's quite a bit of work to do. We've got a lot of apples on one of the trees. I couldn't find that plum tree though. You know the one you picked the plums from that

I had last night? You'll have to show me which one it is.'

As they were turning into the lane from the main road, her father stopped and looked at her. 'It's going to be all right,' he said.

Jess looked at him. It was as if her father was asking her, not telling her.

'Yes,' she said. 'It's going to be all right,' giving him a big smile.

'That's my girl,' he said. 'That's the spirit.'

'You know,' Jess said, as they reached the gate of Lavender Cottage. 'You know, before we moved, you said we were 'going back to our roots?' What are our roots?'

'My goodness, that's a question.' Her father paused with his hand on the cottage gate. 'Well, this cottage belonged to your grandfather and his father and I'm pretty sure his father before him. I think our family has lived here for about one hundred and fifty years.'

'One hundred and fifty years,' Jess said, doing sums in her head. 'That's the eighteen hundred and fifties'.

'Yes,' her father said. 'At least that. I imagine Lavender Cottage was built before then. We must find out. There must be people who know about these things.'

'Mike knows everything there is to know about the Fens,' Jess said seriously.

'Who's Mike?' her father said, teasing her. 'One of your boyfriends?'

'I don't have any boyfriends!'

'What about the blond haired boy who is always running around and falling out of trees.'

'That's Lee. You saw him?'

'I couldn't really miss him. He used to come up to me

and say. "You all right?" Nice little fellow.'

'Oh! His name is Lee. He is Mike's son. And Mike knows all there is to know about the Fens.'

'Does he indeed? Then I think I'd like to meet this Mike.'

For the first time since they had arrived at Lavender Cottage, mum and dad and Jess all sat down round the table in the kitchen to eat together, talking and laughing just like they used to.

'I expect you're hungry after your first day at the College,' her mother said handing her a plate of shepherd's pie. 'Eat this up. I've made a plum crumble, with some of those plums you brought home. And you tell us all about your day.'

It was a lovely meal and though Jess didn't want it to end, she couldn't stop getting full and tired. She must have dozed off at the table because she suddenly realised that her dad was carrying her upstairs to her room. Sleepily she undressed, put on her pyjamas, washed, cleaned her teeth and crawled into bed with Tedder.

'Sleep well, love,' her father popped his head round the door.

'Night, Dad, love you,' she said.

'Love you, too,' came the reply as he went down the stairs.

20

QUESTIONS

ortunately, it was a short week at school. Three days was tiring enough, next week it would be five. But it had been fine and she was starting to make some new friends in her tutor group. Some of them seemed very clever, but Jess looked forward to the challenge of keeping pace with them.

She was looking forward to a Saturday lie in, but when it came to it, she couldn't rest. She went to the window to draw the curtains and let in some fresh air. As she opened the window, she saw Mike's car in the lane and was a little surprised.

'I expect he's taking Old Tom some essential supplies, Tedder,' she said. She snuggled back into bed, but was just too curious. 'Perhaps Lee and Cassie are with him. I think I'll go and find out.'

She dressed hurriedly, grabbed an apple from the kitchen bowl and ran to Old Tom's cottage. As she hurried up the path, she could hear Old Tom's voice.

'I mean, I got fond of the little ol' boy. I used to take him fishing and I think he spent more time in my garden with the fruit trees than he did in his own. He loved the Cox's apples. They should be coming on now. Real English apple! Best if you can keep 'em on the tree as long as possible, then you can put them in store for Christmas.'

'That's what my granddad did,' Mike was sitting opposite Old Tom. She could just see him, but he wasn't looking towards her.

'Digger were a poor old thing. I used to go round and see him and we'd have a smoke and drink or two, but the war had done for him. His mother were there looking after him. That made it difficult for Alice. She'd become, I dunno, bitter, I suppose. It was hard for her. It weren't much of a life, but she doted on her boy.

'She was determined her son was going to get on. "He's going to that Grammar school," she used to say. "Then university. He can get away from the fen and have a proper life. He can do something and go somewhere where he doesn't have to scrimp and save all the time." '

'They only had that one boy. He meant everything to them. But Alice wasn't happy. I did ask her one time why she stuck with Digger. "I made my bed and I shall lie on it," was all she said. Young folks today don't think that, do they? As soon as anything goes wrong, they're off and after a divorce. It was different then.'

'Do you think there's any chance you can find that lad?' Old Tom suddenly said. 'You said I could be a wealthy man. Well, I've always thought I had nothing to leave and no one to leave it to. But I've done a lot of thinking over the last few months. That little ol' boy, Will.' Old Tom dropped his voice and Jess could barely hear him. 'He could have been mine.'

'I wondered at the time, but Alice, she wouldn't say nothing. She was right about him going to the grammar school and I didn't see so much of him then. Though he did come round for a chat and have a wander in the orchard. Digger died around that time, while the boy was finishing grammar school. Once he got up to university he was hardly around at all and he must have stayed away, like she wanted.

'He'd be a grandfather now, most likely but I'd love to know what happened to him. I think about him and wonder where he is. Can you find people? Do you have one of them computers?'

Jess must have moved and Mike had sensed she was near the door. 'It's only me,' she said putting her head round the door, much to Faithful's delight.

'It's the little ol' gal!' said Old Tom looking up. 'How did you get on at school me ol' beauty?'

'It was good, thank you,' she said, feeling a little awkward. She shouldn't have listened in. But she couldn't help thinking about what Old Tom had said.

'There's someone here who'd like a good run along the bank if you'd like to take him.'

Faithful was already by her legs wagging his tail. 'Come on, boy,' she said, glad of a reason to go out. 'See you later,' she called as she set off after Faithful who was already romping ahead of her.

It was lovely along the bank. The air smelled of the fen. Blackberries and blueberries were hanging heavily from the bushes begging to be eaten. She gathered some as she walked while Faithful sniffed along the hedgerow, before darting between her legs and into the bushes.

Her mind was on Old Tom. He had been troubled since the first time she met him and now she knew why. But could it really be true that 'his little ol' boy' was her father? Everything fitted. Alice was his dead mother and his father was called Digger. She hadn't completely understood what Old Tom meant when he said: 'He could have been mine.' But the more she thought about it, the more it seemed likely.

She was so confused. The only thing to do was to take Mike to meet her dad. They would be able to sort it all out. It was definitely something for grown-ups.

Jess had reached the wooden bridge that crossed over the lode into Monks Fen. She stood in the middle of it, first looking back down the Lode where she could make out the roof of Old Tom's cottage in the trees and see the sails of the windmill in Mill Lane to one side of it.

Turning the other way she looked across fen and fields. The line of pylons broke the horizon. Light sparkled off the water of the main river where the Lode ran into it. She could see some people in Monks Fen. 'Bug hunters, Faithful,' she said, as he peered through the railings of the bridge wagging his tail at the ducks below them. 'Such a perfect day for it.'

She tried to imagine her dad when he was her age, standing on this bridge or walking along the bank or sitting quietly fishing.

The weather had been so lovely since she had lived at Fens End, but when it rained, she had watched in wonder as it came rolling down the Lode, turning everything lush shades of green and she loved the way the land steamed when the sun came out again. She couldn't wait to spend a winter here and was hoping that the Lode would freeze over.

I know where I belong. I have found my roots. This is my fen. Our fen. We belong here. She reached down and rubbed Faithful's head.

When she got back to the cottage, Old Tom was enjoying a roll up while Mike was writing in his notebook. 'All right, Mr Fuller, I'll see what I can do for you,' he said noticing Jess and Faithful.

'Catch anything?' Old Tom said to Faithful as he came to rub up against his legs. 'Remember, I haven't got a long time now,' he said looking again towards Mike. 'You'll need to get a bit of a move on. I think that Ol' Dog's coming to call any time now.'

'I hope not yet,' said Mike. 'Look, you take care and don't worry. I'll get back to you as soon as I can.'

As they walked along the bank towards the Lane, Jess said, 'Have you got time to talk to Dad? He would like to meet you.'

'Of course,' said Mike. He was looking thoughtful. 'Yes, I'd love to.'

21

FAMILY MATTERS

So you're the man who knows everything there is to know about the Fens!' Jess's dad reached out to Mike shaking his hand.

'I think,' said Mike with a smile, 'that Sally at the Museum has a lot to answer for, Jess! Let's just say, I know a bit and I'm learning more all the time. You're Jess's father?'

'I know what you are thinking. Jess was a blessing; I think that's the right word. A blessing, that was given to us a little late in life.'

'Well,' said Mike, 'I had four 'blessings' late in life. We have something in common. You haven't been living here long, I gather.'

'No we moved down from Nottingham in early June. But this was my mother and father's cottage. I grew up here.'

'Would you like a cup of coffee or some tea?' her mum asked popping her head round the door.

'Coffee would be lovely, thank you, white, two sugars, please. So, your father was Henry Barnes, known as

'Digger' and your mother was Alice Barnes.'

'You really do know everything, then!' Her father was laughing. 'And I'm William – my nearest and dearest call me Will. I was named after my grandfather, Old Digger.'

Mike's eyes were twinkling. He looked at Jess and winked. 'I think that we've got quite a lot to talk about.'

Mike explained that he had met Jess at Ely Museum and that she had introduced him to Old Tom. 'He's quite a character! Has lots of stories to tell,' said Mike, still twinkling.

'Tom Fuller? Is he still alive? I used to spend hours with him when I was younger! You see my father went blind after the war. So it was his friend, Tom, who taught me to fish and skate. His parents had a wonderful orchard...Ah! Of course, those plums, they came from him?'

Her father looked around for Jess, who was standing quietly in the background. 'Those trees are they still there? He also had the most marvellous Cox's apple trees. They were my favourite. Are they still there too?'

'Yes dad. And it's going to be a good crop this year too,' he says.

'Well, then I must go and see the old boy. And his orchard!'

'There are some matters I'd like to talk over with you first, if that's ok?'

'Of course, of course, it's just that it is all coming back to me. You see, my roots are here. I was just so busy with my business that I never really had any time to keep in touch with it all, especially after my mother died.'

'Tell me about Alice,' said Mike as he sipped his coffee.

'My mum? She wasn't one to talk a lot. She was an attractive girl. Dark eyes and dark hair, typical fen girl.

I think several of the local lads were after her. But then along came the war. Of course, she married dad, but I always thought she had a soft spot for Tom Fuller.

'She told me once that she fell in love with an American flier. She said he was a lovely young lad and that he was going to marry her and take her back to America with him when the war was over. You can imagine it, can't you? A young girl who had grown up in Fens End, never been much further than Cambridge or a day at the sea at Hunstanton. And there she was being offered a whole new life in a whole new world. America! So glamorous and exciting. A place she'd seen on the films at the Rex in Ely or the Regent in Soham.'

'I've no doubt she was in love with this lad, though. Then one day one of his pals turned up and told her that he was 'missing presumed killed.' The flying fortress he was in had gone down in flames over Germany. People so easily forget the sacrifices those young men made. Just go to Madingley War Cemetery and you'll know what the war did to those young men, so far from their homes too.'

He sounds like Old Tom talking about his war, thought Jess.

'When he died I think she was on the rebound, as they say. All she would say to me was, 'I made a mistake, but I made my bed and I had to lie on it.' I'm not sure if Digger was my father, or someone else. It wasn't the American lad, I know that. But she found herself pregnant with me. People talked in a small village, so when Digger came home on a short leave, they married. They had no home of their own, so she moved in here with Digger's parents. Digger was wounded shortly after D-Day and brought back to this country. He spent a while in hospital, but he came back here just in time for me to be born, which was in the January of 1945.'

'Now, his mother was Caroline. She had been a Butcher, before she married Old Digger. She was a strong woman. She needed to be. Old Digger, like a lot of old fen boys, wasn't easy to live with. He'd stay out all night on the fen poaching to put something in the pot or make a bit of money. A woman's life was hard enough as it was. Of course, when dad came home she wanted to look after him, take care of her son.'

'You can imagine what was going on. Alice wasn't an easy woman either. She'd had a hard enough life before and then she'd hardly had any married life with Digger before he came home injured. Now she had Grandma Barnes doing everything for him and nothing for Alice. I was about seventeen when Dad died. I think that just about killed Grandma, because not long after she also died.'

'Alice spent most of her time looking after me. I'm sure she had wanted to look after her husband, as well. He was one hundred per cent disabled. That gave them enough money to manage on, but she often reminded me how they had to 'scrimp and save'. She was very ambitious for me. I got into Soham Grammar School and from there she wanted me to go to university and get away from the fen. She said there were no opportunities around here.'

'She often told me that I was the only thing in her life that mattered to her and I was desperate not to let her down. I worked hard, got some decent A Levels and I was accepted at Nottingham University. As luck would have it, I met my business partner at university and we set up a manufacturing business in Nottingham and we were very successful. I married and then Jess came along.' He sighed deeply, shrugging his shoulders and rolling his head to loosen his neck, before he continued in a lower, sadder voice.

'You know we really did have everything. It was mum that pushed me so I could do that. Then when the business got into trouble, I really believed we could save it. We had creditors; people owed us a lot of money. But they were in trouble too and the banks wouldn't support us while we waited for things to get better and that was that. A lot of good men lost their jobs. We had to sell everything and move here.'

'We were lucky we still had the cottage. We'd been letting it out, so it was in a good enough state that we could move in.'

Jess was sitting quietly in the corner of the room. She daren't speak or draw attention to herself, or they might send her out to play, as adults often did when there were things they thought she shouldn't hear. But she wanted to hear this. She wanted to know about her grandma and her granddad and where Old Tom fitted into their lives.

'Well, you are back now, that's for sure. Back to your roots,' Mike said. 'And back to Tom Fuller.' Mike leaned forward and looked at her Dad, pausing before he spoke. 'He seems to think that you could be his son.'

Jess held her breath. Her dad seemed frozen to the spot, his breathing shallow, his eyes wide with disbelief.

'What has he said to you?'

'He told me that while he was on leave before D-Day he met Alice along the lode bank and that she and him...' Mike trailed off and suddenly Jess knew that they both realised she was in the room.

'Jess, love, go and see what your mother is up to. Another coffee, Mike? You'll have another coffee, won't you and I'll join you. Jess go and ask your mother for a couple of coffees please, will you? Then go and play outside for a while.'

'But, dad!' Jess really wanted to stay, but the look on her dad's face told her that she really should go and ask her mum to make the coffees. She sidled out of the room as slowly as she possibly could, desperate to hear more.

As Jess went through the door, she heard her father say, 'Somehow I'm not surprised, by this,' his voice sounding thick and strange. 'I'm not surprised at all.'

22

WILL

The cottage door was half open as always. Jess often thought she should tell him to keep the door locked and that he should be more careful because anyone could just wander in. But then she thought that was how she had first met him and anyway it would be a waste of time. She called out as she reached it. 'Mr Fuller, are you there?'

Faithful came to the door to greet her as she heard Old Tom's reply, 'Well, I ain't gone to church this morning, though I should have done, it being a Sunday an all. Couldn't find me collar stud.' He chuckled. One of his jokes, Jess thought.

'I've brought someone to see you.' Behind Jess her father was fidgeting, she could sense his nervousness. She stepped inside the cottage and her father followed her. 'It's my Dad,'she said, 'I think you used to know him.'

The old man peered up at the tall figure coming into the room. 'Come over more into the light,' he said. 'So I can get a proper look at you.'

'William Barnes,' her father said, 'You used to call me Will. It's been a long time.'

The old man didn't speak for a while. 'Is it really you?' he eventually said. 'Only sometimes I sit here and I sort of dream people are here, you know, people I used to know. Then I suddenly wake up and there's no one here.'

'I'm really here and this is my daughter, Jess, I think you've seen quite a lot of her this summer.'

'This little ol' gal, is your little ol' gal?' Old Tom was looking from one to the other. 'I don't rightly know what to say. Look, sit you down.' He fumbled for his tobacco pouch and papers. He rolled a cigarette and lit it. He wiped his eyes. 'Blast, bit of smoke must have got in them,' he said and then gathering himself he added: 'It's going to be a good year for Cox's, you always liked them best of all.'

'I certainly did!' Her father looked round the cluttered room. 'The old place hasn't changed much.'

'No need, it suits me. It'll see me out. Now I want to know all about you and what has brought you back to Fens End.'

'Come on, Faithful,' Jess said. 'I think they've got a lot of catching up to do. Time for a walk.'

They were still talking when Jess got back to the cottage, so she went through to the orchard to see what ripe fruit there was.

23

MAKING PLANS

I still can't believe it all,' her father was saying again. 'I thought the old fellow would be dead by now.' It was later that same day and the evening was warm. Jess was sitting with her mum and dad by the back door.

He turned to Jess, 'Your Mike has told him that he could be a very wealthy man. And now he wants to leave it all to us when he dies. He asked me to sort out a will and everything as soon as possible. He's very taken with you. He calls you his 'little ol' gal' and he wants you to be well looked after.'

'I am well looked after,' Jess said looking puzzled.

'He's not talking about us and how much we love you! He knows that. He knows that I lost the business and we've got very little money coming in. And he wants to help to put us back on our feet again. He was very insistent about getting a solicitor straight away. He kept telling me I mustn't leave it too long.'

'He's seen the Old Black Dog,' Jess said.

'What Old Black Dog?' her mum asked.

'Old Black Shuck. It's a big black hound with eyes as big as saucers, if you see it, it means death to you or death in the family within twelve months, that's what they say...'

'Jess, really! It's that Mike and his stories again, isn't it?'

'Yes, but Old Tom's seen it and so have I.'

'If you've seen a big black dog wandering loose around here, we ought to report it.'

'Oh, mum, it's just that I know what it means. You must see that lawyer tomorrow, Dad.'

'I will, love, I will. Just think what this means though. When anything happens to Old Tom his cottage and a huge parcel of land would belong to us. Some of it could be sold so we could spend some money on doing up the cottage, or this one. We would have money to spend on the boat house.'

'We could do holiday lets, give people boat trips down the Lode, probably not in that punt that's down there, though. We've got enough old fen tools and bits and pieces to start our own museum. We'll have to get Mike to come out here and tell us what everything is.'

'Why is he doing this for us?' Jess asked.

'We're like his family, love.' She saw a little look flicker between her mum and dad.

'You mean you could be his son. And that would make me his granddaughter.'

'Jess!' Her mother and father exclaimed in unison.

'Well, he might be. He is. Isn't he?'

Another look passed between her mum and her dad, and Jess saw her mum sigh and nod.

'He does look on you as his granddaughter. It's nice for

him to think that he has family to pass everything on to,'
said her Dad.

Jess liked the idea of Old Tom as her grandfather. She
had already spent more time with him than she had any of
her other grandparents.

She lay in bed that night thinking of what she would say
to Marcie Whitworth if ever their paths should cross again.
'Yes I was poor for a while, but now I'm rich again, richer
than you can ever imagine and I'm not just talking about
money.'

As she fell asleep she thought of Granddad Tom in his
little cottage, of Faithful curled up asleep and somewhere
out on Lode Bank, that old Black Dog with the sad eyes
waiting.

24

LEGAL AND BINDING

As her father had promised, he had acted straight away and a local solicitor visited Old Tom the very next morning.

Old Tom said he couldn't read what had been written down as he couldn't find his glasses, but he had listened carefully as the will had been read back to him. 'Now, you're sure, 'everything has gone to Will, his wife and my little ol' gal?'

'Absolutely, Mr Fuller, according to your wishes.'

'And that's all proper, all legal and binding like?'

'It certainly is, once you have signed it.'

Old Tom had taken the pen and had signed his name with some difficulty. 'I haven't got my glasses, you see,' he kept explaining. 'Will that do?' he looked up at the solicitor.

'Well we're now going to countersign to say that's exactly what it will do. Mr Rouse, is it? Perhaps you could sign as witness here and put your address.'

'Thank you,' the old man said to Mike, who had brought more supplies. 'And thank you for all the essential bits and bobs you've been bringing out to me. I must owe you a few bob and I haven't left you anything. You'll have to talk to Will here and my little ol' gal and they'll see you right when anything happens to me.'

'That won't be for a long time, yet, Mr Fuller,' he had said.

Jess listened to the account of the day's events. It was still tea time, not too late. 'I'll be back soon,' she said running out of Lavender Cottage before anyone could stop her.

The cottage was quiet. The door was half open. Jess stopped on the path. Suddenly she was unsure. She went forward cautiously. 'Granddad,' she called. *Why had she said that?* She looked in the room. The chair by the fire place was empty. Everywhere was quiet. All she could hear was the old clock solemnly ticking.

She went a little further into the room. 'Granddad? Mr Fuller?' she called again.

Suddenly Faithful came bounding in from the scullery. 'Is that my little ol' gal,' a voice came from near the back door. 'Were you worried about me? I've just been getting a couple of fresh eggs for my tea.'

Jess stood and looked as the old man came in to the room. 'I'm going to boil these and have some bread and butter with them.'

'Would you like me to do them for you?' she said.

'Well, that'd be very kind of you. You'll find a pan out there. Mind you nothing's too clean, but I shan't come to no harm now, I don't suppose. Go and fetch yourself a couple of eggs, there'll be some out there and you can join me.'

'How long do you boil them for? Jess called out from the scullery.

'About four minutes will do for me, thank you. Though sometimes I forget and get hard boiled eggs.'

'Just the job,' the old man said, finishing his eggs. 'Can't beat a freshly laid egg and getting waited on hand and foot. Can't be bad, eh? I suppose you'd better run along home, they'll be wondering where you've got to.'

Jess went over and gave the old man a peck on the cheek. 'Night granddad,' she said.

'Night, my ol' beauty,' he said. 'Now don't you go worrying yourself about me.'

Jess ran home. 'Just been to see Granddad,' she said as she came through the door.

25

STRUGGLING SHADOWS

I t was a lovely Autumn. Jess's first in the Fens, and she loved the way the bright green gave way to the gold and yellows and browns. Blackberries still hung on the bushes, but by now the witches had spat on them, so they tasted bitter.

'Jessica Barnes, where do you get this nonsense from!' her mum had said. 'Don't tell me. Mike or Old Tom.'

'Ah, Old Sally, he won't catch her!' Old Tom had chuckled when Jess was telling him how Faithful had chased a big rabbit with enormous ears until the dog was worn out and panting.

'Do you know her?' Jess was puzzled.

'That was a hare, not so many of them around these days. We used to call them Old Sally, as witches used to change into hares so they could have a look around or get away from anyone who wanted to dunk 'em in the village pond. Just fetch me that little box on the shelf over there.'

She did as he asked and took him the box, watching him as he fumbled around in the few bits of coins and things inside and then handed her a smooth stone. 'What do you think of that, then?'

'It's a stone,' Jess said puzzled, 'with a hole in it.'

'That was my father's safe-keep from witches.'

'Your father saw witches?' Jess asked wide eyed.

'Course he didn't,' the old man chuckled, 'he was carrying that stone!'

Old Tom seemed very happy. He was always pleased to see her, but he wasn't as strong as he was when they had first met. Her mother was cooking meals for him and Jess was taking them round most days. Her father would sit and talk with him about the old days for ages.

One day, Mr Julian Russell-Shaw turned up on the doorstep with his colleague. Jess was sitting by the pond watching a dragon fly hovering and darting about. She heard her father from inside the cottage. 'I think you have already been told that Mr Fuller has no wish to sell. Who am I? I'm Mr Fuller's son.'

Jess couldn't hear what Mr Russell-Shaw said. She could hear her father's voice though and it was just like how he used to be back in Nottingham when he was dealing with business matters. 'You must have been misinformed, Mr Russell-Shaw. Mr Fuller does have a family. I am his son and the young lady out there, is my daughter, his grand daughter. And, what is more, we are well aware of how much my father's land might be worth. If we need to talk to you, we will be in touch. Thank you.'

Jess watched the two men in suits depart along the tow path. She could hear Old Tom, laughing loudly. 'That told 'em! Well done, son. When I'm gone, you do what you think best for yourself and my little ol' gal. Pity to sell the old orchard though, it's been one of the best years I can remember for fruit. Have you had a look lately, I reckon you can go and pick some Cox's now. It's October. You remember how to tell if they're really ripe don't you?'

Her father knew. 'With a Cox's orange pippin, they start to turn this lovely, reddy, orangy colour and when you shake them you should be able to hear the pips rattle. Jess!' her father called. 'Come on, I'll introduce you to a real English apple.'

Jess got up and followed her father through the cottage. Old Tom was watching. 'You bring some for me, now,' he said.

Jess picked one, she held it to her ear and shook it. The pips rattled. She took a bite and as it crunched and the juice hit her mouth, she knew in that moment what her father and Old Tom had been talking about. 'Oh, wow!'

'Now that,' said her father holding out a half eaten one, 'is what I call an apple.'

'Here you are, granddad,' she said, as she placed some apples in his lap. Old Tom got out his shut knife and began slicing pieces off one. 'I know autumn's arrived when I taste these,' he said. 'Real English apple. Now you pick as many sound ones as you can over the next week or so, wrap them up in newspaper and store them somewhere cool and dry and you'll be eating these on Christmas Day.'

That night she went up to her bedroom nice and early. It had been a lovely day with so much to think about. She looked along her shelves to find a book to read in bed.

She had only been in the fens a few months, but so much had happened. Her father had been ill and then got better, she had met Mike, she had found that she had a granddad.

They had been poor and now they had, like Pip, 'Great Expectations...'

She looked at the book that Lee and Cassie had brought her for her birthday in July. She was embarrassed to think that she had not read it yet. She opened it, it was also signed by Ben and Lauren and she hadn't met them yet. Mike knew how much she loved reading and was always talking about books to her. 'The Ghosts of Blacklode' by John Gordon. He was the same author that had written 'Fen Runners'. Mike said he was the best. She thought that she would just read a little bit before she went to sleep.

It was the fens. It was winter and Bill had stamped on the ice of Bell Creek and chanted: 'If she cracks she bears; if she bends she breaks.

So that's where Mike gets some of his stories and sayings from, she thought.

She lay the book down on her duvet for a minute and looked up at the low ceiling of her room. Above that ceiling were centuries of thatch in which small creatures probably slept. Across the darkened lane in the old farmyard Mr Cock-a-Doodle-Do kept watch over his hens until morning light when he would wake them and her.

Down by the still dark waters of the lode, Old Tom, granddad, would be asleep in his little cottage with Faithful curled up close by. Out on the fen the creatures of the night would be about their business, while others would be nestled away until dawn.

And somewhere out there along that bank a big Old Black Dog was waiting.

It was getting late and she was tired, but she just wanted to listen to something again. She found her birthday CD and put it on the little player beside her bed. She found the track she wanted. It was one of John's songs, 'Between the Flatland and the Sky'.

She listened carefully.

'Down to earth ploughline and seedtime,
Watching the river roll by,
Down to earth harvest and moonshine'
Between the flatland and the sky...'

That could have been written for Old Tom and all the fenmen like him. John was singing about 'where our histories lie' and this is where her history lay, she knew that now.

And then towards the end of the song:

'We struggling shadows, born to die here with earth on our hands,
Between the flatland and the sky.'

That was Old Digger and Young Digger, Nanna Alice, Old Toms' parents Joseph and Sarah and all those old fen men who had gone before. All struggling shadows...

As she fell asleep the book slid off the bed and dropped to the floor.

26

HALF TERM

That half term Jess spent as much time as she could with her granddad. He sat and talked to her about when he was young.

'Times were hard,' he would say. 'The old fens were changing. The old turf diggers, and wildfowlers were part of a dying way of life.'

'I knew it wouldn't last, I suppose, that's why I took the different work I could when I left school. Father had already got a job with the River Board. Some of the old boys like my grandfather, hardly ever left the fen, but by the time I was your age, there were cars on the roads. But the thing I loved best were the talking pictures. Now I did think that were something amazing. My old dad had seen the old silent pictures at Nick Nack Taylor's cinema in Soham and the first time we saw the 'talkies' as they were called, he couldn't get over it.'

'The first time I saw a talking picture was in The Rex at Ely. That was a lovely picture house and theatre as well, because they used to have acts come on the stage between the films. For a little old boy such as me from out of the fen, sitting there in those red plush seats, with all the carpets and lights, it was magic. For just a tanner I was taken out of the old fen to London, America, all over the world. I just thought it was wonderful. I could get a bag of chips at the fish and chip shop and I thought I was a lord for a day.'

Then there was the wireless. We didn't have one, but I remember one of my friends built a crystal set as he called it. Now that were something, listening to voices and music coming out of a little box.'

'Did you have a television?' Jess asked one time.

'Television? Bless you, no. First television I ever saw was in the Rendezvous Club at Soham. That was some time after the war. Little ol' black and white screen that flickered and kept crackling when a car went by and flipped over and over if an aeroplane flew over. Didn't think that would ever catch on.'

Jess loved listening to his tales with Faithful curled up between them. 'When anything happens to me, you will look after the ol' dog, won't you? He gets on well with you,' Old Tom said often.

'Of course, I will,' she said. 'You know I will, but nothing...'

'Jess, now listen, something will happen to me one of these days. That Ol' Black Dog will come for me soon, and I'm ready. I've had a good life. I've done what I could and best of all I've found my family. I know that when I've gone, you'll all look after everything. That's all a man needs, you know.'

Sometimes Old Tom would doze off in his chair. 'Alice, Alice?' He once called out. Jess froze, she didn't know what to say. 'Where are you, Alice?'

What dreams was he having? Jess knew that Old Tom had loved Alice and that Alice was her Dad's mother and Old Tom was her Dad's father. She knew that and one day when she was a writer, she would write a story about a young man and a young girl who were separated by war and could never get back together again. The thought of the story made her sad.

She wanted to ask old Tom about Bergen-Belsen and what he saw. After all she had heard about the Holocaust at school and she had read some of Anne Frank's Diary. But Old Tom wouldn't say much.

'There are some things, my little ol' gal, you'd best not know too much about,' he used to say. 'I saw things that human beings had done to other human beings, that were worse than anything I'd ever seen. It's up to you young people to make sure that nothing like that ever happens again.'

More happily Old Tom would talk about the fights the boys would get in to, especially with the Soham boys. 'There were some rough ol' boys,' he used to say. 'They would have a scrap just for the fun of it, like boys today might kick a football around. We had to make our own entertainment and having a bit of a scrap, we thought was good fun.'

One morning when she called round Old Tom was eating something from a small bowl. 'Just made myself a bowl of sop,' he said with a grin. 'Just fancied it and I had some pieces of bread.'

'Sop? What's that?'

'You never had water or milk sop? My old mother used to give it to me all the time when I was young and there wasn't much food in the house. You get a basin like this, he held up the small chipped basin in his hand and you break up three or four slices of bread in it. Then you pour on some boiling water, just enough to make the bread moist but not soggy, then you cover it with a plate so the steam moistens the bread. You can leave that for about three minutes, then you take off the plate and you mash up the bread with a spoon. It looks a bit revolting, but then you add a good amount of butter and pepper and salt to taste and mash it all up well. Then you eat it while it's nice and hot. Lovely on a cold day.'

The look on Jess's face told Tom that she wasn't going to try it. 'You could make it with milk instead of water and don't season it, just a little butter perhaps. No? Still don't fancy it? Ah well, you don't need to eat nothing like that these days, we had to make do with what we had.'

'Mother would make a lot of steamed puddings in the boiler. Sometimes she would put meat in one end and then have a suet stopper in the middle and jam at the other end. How about that? Main meal and pudding all at the same time?' He chuckled.

'I feel sorry for the women years ago. They had hard lives. They brought up the children in little old cottages, that were damp. There was no electric light, no running water inside, unless the roof leaked and it was raining. Some of the cottages had pumps, a lot got their water from the rivers or drains.

'We also had a water butt out the back and my father always used to wash in water from that, 'Lovely soft water,' he would say. I used to do it too, it was lovely.'

'On a Friday night, father would get down the old tin bath, I've still got it somewhere out the back. He'd put it on the floor here in front of the fire if it were winter time. That would be filled with hot water and the children would be bathed one after the other. With some big families the last one in would come out dirtier than he started. We didn't do too badly being only the two of us.'

Sometimes, if Old Tom fell asleep while she was there, she would stand and watch to see his chest rise and fall, to make sure that he was just sleeping. Sometimes she would just sit there with nothing to break the silence but the lovely deep tick of the grandfather clock in the corner. It was just like one of the family, standing there watching everyone, telling the time, counting the days, the weeks, the months, the years.

When he woke they would have an apple each. Out would come his shut knife and somehow he would peel the skin off in one long spiral, before popping chunks of apple in his mouth. 'These were your father's favourites,' he would say.

'They still are,' Jess would say and Old Tom would smile. 'Well make sure you've got plenty in store, you'll not buy as good. Nothing like eating something from your own garden. We allus used to grow our own vegetables too. Nothin' like the first crop of runner beans or peas or lovely new potatoes. And there's nothing like a bit of sparrow's grass cut straight from the garden and boiled and eaten with just a knob of butter.

'Sparrow's grass?'

'Asparagus, of course! You ought to start growing some things, my ol' gal. You're a country girl now.'

That's just what I am, thought Jess, as she walked home that evening. 'I'm an ol' Fen gal,' she said aloud in the best imitation she could manage of Old Tom's accent.

27

FEN SUNSET

The weather in late October was beautiful and the sunsets were stunning, with blood reds and pinks and golds filling the sky. She loved her new school and was doing well, but escaping in the fresh air and walking along the lode with Faithful cleared her head of the hustle and bustle of the day and enabled her to think.

She would be a writer. She knew she had stories to tell. And out here, she felt that anything and everything was possible.

Old Tom seemed to be getting more tired as they got to the end of the week. He was always pleased to see her or her dad, and he was happy to talk and tell his stories, but he would fall asleep and then sometimes find it difficult to realise where he was again.

One evening as Jess was leaving, Old Tom levered himself out of his armchair and followed her out into the front garden. The sun was setting across the Fen and reflecting off the Lode.

'I'm glad I lived here, and my father and grandfather along this bank and I don't know how many Fullers before them. I ain't seen much of other places, except during the war when they weren't at their best. I went to Hunstanton a few times and Yarmouth, but that were a bit too crowded for me. I suppose I was happy here. I love the Fens. That ain't a bad thing, is it? I mean to know where you belong and be happy with it.'

Jess looked at his old wrinkled face. His eyes were watery. 'And I'm the luckiest man in the world.' He looked at her. 'You came into my life one day and now I have my granddaughter to leave everything to. I know, you're a clever little ol' gal, you've been listening to things and you understand a lot.'

'I was having such a lovely dream,' he said one afternoon to Jess. ' I 'm walking along the Lode bank and there is Alice coming to meet me, just as I remember her, all dark hair and flashing eyes, full of mischief. Sometimes my mother and father are waiting for us down the end of the path where the Lode turns into the main river. We were all going to be together again and just as we all got close together, I woke up. But I want it to carry on. They're waiting for me.'

Jess looked at his tired old face, his eyes were moist and he fumbled for a handkerchief. 'Listen to me, silly old fool, eh?'

'No, granddad,' she said, 'no, you're not.' She went over to him and gave him a big hug and kissed his stubbly cheek. 'Love, you.'

He looked at her. 'Do you know?' he said. 'I never hugged my grandfather or kissed him or my grandmother, or my father or mother. I never told them how much I loved them. I wish I had. I suppose we didn't in those days. I'm pleased it's different now. I love you too, little ol' gal. You enjoy your life, now, and don't worry about me. I shall be all right.'

As she went out of the cottage door that evening, she looked back and Old Tom gave her one of his little smiles and a small wave of hand. She watched him for a while from the doorway as he rolled a cigarette and poured himself a drop of whisky, tipping the bottle up until it was empty.

'Just the job,' he said. 'Lovely little drop of whisky. Just for medicinal purposes, of course.' He raised the tumbler, 'God Bless,' he said.

That evening the sun was setting in a blaze of glory over the fen. Jess was in the front garden of Lavender Cottage enjoying the still quite warm autumn evening. Suddenly she found herself running towards the Lode bank.

As she turned onto the path beside the Lode the setting sun and the reflection off the Lode was dazzling. Jess stopped and tried to adjust her eyes. The sky was blood red.

Walking towards the setting sun she could see Old Tom walking better than ever she had seen him walk. Beside him was a huge hound. As she got closer to his cottage, Faithful was crouched on the path looking towards them. As Jess drew next to him he looked at her and gave a little whimper.

'It's all right, boy,' she said. 'It's all right.'

She knelt beside him and put her arm down to stroke him and together they watched the old man and the Ol' Black Dog get further and further away until they disappeared.

28

A THURSDAY IN EARLY NOVEMBER

It was a lovely little service in the small church in the village. It was a beautiful autumn morning. As the Vicar talked about Old Tom the sun had shone through the stained glass windows creating puddles of jewelled light on the stone floor.

The churchyard, dappled with the reds and golds of fallen leaves, was full of Fullers and Baileys and Bullmans and Barnes. Old Tom was going home.

Some of the old villagers had turned out. 'All in their Sunday best' as her Mum remarked. 'I'm glad they've come.'

After the service, everyone came back to Lavender Cottage and warmed themselves against the chill of the autumn afternoon with cups of tea and sandwiches and cake. Old people Jess had never seen before chatted about what a character Old Tom had been, with conversations punctuated by gusts of laughter.

Jess found Mike sitting in the garden admiring the roses that were still in full bloom.

He looked at her and smiled. ' Well, Jess, I don't suppose you are going to need me much now Old Tom has gone and your dad is well again.' He looked a little sad.

Jess looked at him and then gave him a hug. 'Of course I need you. You know...'

'...everything there is to know about the fens! I know. Well, I'll let you into a little secret, I don't. But I've learnt a great deal more from Old Tom and you've learnt an awful lot yourself this summer. You're a proper ol' fen gal now.' He stood to leave.

Faithful came rubbing against her legs and looked up at her with sad eyes. 'It's alright, boy,' she said, rubbing his ears, 'I'll look after you. How about a walk, just you and me along the bank and see the sunset? I don't think we'll see that Ol' Black Dog this evening.'

Mike smiled. 'You've certainly found your roots, little o' gal,' he said softly, as he watched Jess and Faithful set out alongside the dark waters of the Lode towards where the fen stretched out for miles and miles under the glowing sky.

A FEN GLOSSARY

A NOTE ON THE FEN DIALECT

The old Fen dialect is dying out with the influence of more education and the media. Old Fen folk who confused 'was' and 'were', and who shortened 'that's' to 'thass', are these days few and far between (or, rather, 'atween'); as a result many of the old words and expressions peculiar to the Fens have also been lost. Here is an explanation of some of the words and phrases, which were once in common usage in the Cambridgeshire Fens.

Acrorst - across

Ain't (also **int** and **een't**) - isn't

Allus - always

Atween - between

Biler - the boiler where you heated water, boiled your puddens and washed your clothes

Black Shuck - a big dog, with eyes like saucers (often red) who, if encountered on some Fen bank, meant there would be death to you or in the family within the twelve months

Bog Oaks - trees buried in the fen **peat,** (see below) black wood hard as iron and not necessarily oak

Boggarts - mischief makers, out there in the dark Fen

Bogles (see also **Boggarts**) - you wouldn't wait around to tell the difference, but they are nastier little imps

Bor- boy - an 'old bor' could be as young as twelve

Bucket and Chuck it - a relatively sophisticated toilet arrangement, with an outhouse at the back of the cottage, a wooden bench seat and a door that opened to reveal a bucket, the contents of which would be buried

Bruck - a broken or broke, e.g. 'I bruck my ol shovel.'

Brung - brought, as in: 'Ol' Dusty brung me a goose.'

Cack-handed - clumsy

Contraption - an all purpose word for anything from a piece of machinery to an old car, suggesting it looks cobbled together.

Dab Hand - someone clever at doing something.

Dead Hand - this would come out of the bog or marsh and grab you and pull you under.

Ding - a sharp blow, as in 'I cheeked the policemen and got a ding round the lug ole.'

Dipping Hole – a hole bruck in the ice of the river or drain, so you could draw water.

Dockey - a morning break for agricultural workers, often bread, cheese and onion, with cold water or cold tea to drink. When you were eating it, your master 'docked' your pay. You weren't paid for taking a break, so it was dockey time.

Drownded - what happened to you if you fell in a Fen drain or river : you got drownded. (see **Hooky Man** below)

Earth closet - basic toilet a hole in the ground covered by a small shed-like structure. There were one-holers and two-holers, which had a smaller hole for smaller bottoms. A nail in the side was a useful addition for hanging torn paper on.

Eel - once caught in their thousands in the Fens. Credited with healing powers, possibly as it is such a mysterious creature spawning in the Sargasso Sea across the Atlantic.

Fen ague (pronounced a-gew) - a form of malaria common in the marshy Fens.

Fen Blow - when the dry soil, often in early spring, is blown like a sand storm into the next county by the wind.

Fen runners or **patins** - fen skates.

Fen slodger - an old fen wildfowler.

Fen Tiger - a native of the Fens.

Foller - follow

Frawn, Frorn or Fruzz - the ground was frozen.

Glaive (usually pronounced gleeve, so sometimes spelt gleave) four (usually) barbed tines on a long handle for spearing eels through the water and mud.

Grigg - long willow basket narrow at both end, baited for trapping eels , also called a **hive**.

Grut - great or big, as in: 'Look at that grut ol' bor.'

Handy Woman - probably elderly woman who acted as nurse, midwife and undertaker. (see **Wise Woman**)

Hard water - frozen water not solid enough to skate on.

Hive - an alternative name for eel **grigg**

Hooky Man - Ol' Hooky Man was waiting in fen dykes and rivers to pull you down into a watery grave.

Horkey - harvest feast or celebration.

Hungin - onion

Int - isn't, as in: 'that int fair.'

Keeler or Killer - a wooden trough where the pig that you kept on scraps was killed to provide meat for the winter.

Kettle Broth - see **Water Mess**

Milk Mess - stale bread mashed up in boiled milk. Usually given to the boys as they had to grow up big and strong, girls often got **Water Mess** (see below).

Ol' Gel - Fenman's dear wife or missus.

Oont - won't, as in: 'I oont be gooin to school today.'

Over Will's Mother's - somewhere in the distance.

Paigles - cowslips

Palaver - a fuss, as in: 'there's bin a roight ol' palaver about the state of the village green.'

Patins - skates, Fen word, probably from the French.

Peat - rich, black soil, revealed when the Fens were drained, a kind of compost made from rotting vegetation.

Pingle - to pick at your food.

Poppy Head Tea - made from opium poppies and drunk to cure the **Fen ague,** sometimes used to help a baby sleep.

Privvy - toilet, often basic and at the bottom of the garden (see **earth closet**). Those without a privvy went 'broadcast' in the fields around the cottage.

Pudden - Fen people ate a lot of puddings that could be boiled in the boiler.

Punt gun - a long barrelled gun fitted on a punt, filled with shot and packed with gun powder, might kill sixty or more wildfowl with one huge blast.

Rum ol' doo – a strange event or affair.

Safe Keeps - lucky charms. (see **Boggarts** and **Bogles**)

Slub - wet mud.

Stun - stone

Taters - potatoes; boiled, they made many a meal.

Thass a Davil - expression of some surprise.

Thumb Bit - when your hands were dirty working in the fields, you held your bread between finger and thumb and eat all round it, then threw away the dirty 'thumb bit'.

War Ag - War Agricultural Executive Committee. There was one for every county to increase war time food production.

Water Mess, or salt and pepper sop - stale bread, soaked in hot water, mashed up with salt, pepper and butter to taste.

Water Wallopers - boiled suet or flour puddings

Weren't - wasn't, as in: 'I weren't there.'

Weskit - a waistcoat, popularly worn by boys and men.

Whull - whole, as in: 'a whull hustle of kids.' (a large family)

Wise Woman - Doctor's cost money, so you probably went to the Wise Woman for some herbal cures.

ABOUT THE AUTHOR

Michael Rouse is an historian and the author of some thirty books, many of them photographic. Born in Ely, he has had a lifelong love of the Fens. Since working with groups of children at Ely Museum, he has wanted to tell something of the fenland history in a story. 'Fens End' is his first novel for children.

Acknowledgements

My grateful thanks to Susan Harrison for editing my original story and all her help with the production of this book and Annabel Reddick of Burrows Bookshop for encouragement. My thanks to Sally Austin, the Education Officer at Ely Museum, without whom I wouldn't have become so involved with Fen storytelling, and John Crowe, writer, songwriter and performer, for permission to quote from 'Beyond the Flat Land and the Sky', one of his many songs.

Sally and John are mentioned in this story, while two of my children, Lee and Cassie, make guest appearances as characters that they will no doubt deny bear any resemblance to them. Several of the figures mentioned in the story like Percy Burrows, Mr Walling, the schoolmaster, and the skating champions were real people, as with any members of my family mentioned, but Jess and her family, past and present, Tom Fuller and his family are all invented characters.

My thanks to Maxine and Phil Ward for proof reading. The cover photograph was taken at Wicken Fen, thanks to the National Trust. Special thanks to my daughters: Cassie for being photographed and to Lauren for her help with the design.